USA TODAY bestselling author **Catherine Mann** has won numerous awards for her novels, including both a prestigious RITA® Award and an *RT Book Reviews* Reviewers' Choice Award. After years of moving around the country bringing up four children, Catherine has settled in her home state of South Carolina, where she's active in animal rescue. For more information, visit her website, catherinemann.com.

To Haley and Maggie

Chapter One

Though she be but little, she is fierce.

The quote from Shakespeare's *A Midsummer Night's Dream* echoed through Susanna Levine's brain, bolstering her every step as she stomped through the autumn forest.

She might have a problem standing up for herself, but when it came to the students in her care as a librarian? She could battle a lion.

Lucky for her, there weren't any lions in Moonlight Ridge, Tennessee, mountain home of the Top Dog Dude Ranch. There was just one very annoying parent of a first-grade boy who was struggling with reading. How many notes did she have to send home in little Benji Fuller's planner before she got an answer? How many emails? And the phone number on file wasn't even correct.

Well, she wasn't that easily deterred. She'd dug around in Benji's records and learned that his father owned the construction company in charge of the expansion at the local guest ranch. With each step along the dirt path through the thick forest, the sounds grew louder—roaring engines, jackhammers and the beeping construction equipment in reverse.

Thank goodness she had reinforcements to support her. Her shaggy little pup, Atlas, trotted alongside her, his black-and-white fur rippling in the autumn breeze. And her friend Hollie O'Brien kept pace on her other side. Hollie and her husband, Jacob, were the owners and founders of the Top Dog Dude Ranch.

Susanna adjusted her hold on the leash, even though Atlas wasn't a tugger. He accompanied her to school to provide therapeutic support to the kids. There hadn't been time to take him home, but she couldn't risk his running loose in the woods or in the work area. "Hollie, thank you for walking with me. I'm sorry to pull you away from work."

"It's no trouble at all," her friend said, stuffing her hands into the pockets of her Top Dog Dude Ranch jacket, her dark ponytail swishing. "It's easier to show you where Micah Fuller is than to give directions. Besides, if you don't mind, I'd like to pick your brain on books to recommend to my little girl. I'm still getting to know her preferences."

Hollie and Jacob were adopting four siblings. They were adorable kids, but learning the routine for that many at once still had to be a lot to adjust to, especially while running a growing business.

"Of course I can put together a suggested reading list. But it feels like Ivy has plowed through most of what's in our library. She's consistently reading at least three levels ahead, which makes it a challenge to find stories at her academic level while also being engaging for her chronological age." Susanna fished her phone out from her crossbody bag, adding another item to her to-do list app.

And it made her heart hurt all the more for Benji, who was the same age and lagging so far behind with his reading. Images of his freckled little face filling her mind and fueling her steps, she stomped faster, her sneakers snapping twigs underfoot.

The trail was marked with wooden arrows and

signs shaped like paw prints. Forks in the path were decorated with bales of hay and pumpkins. Another sported a scarecrow pointing toward the stables. The Top Dog Dude Ranch billed itself as the go-to spot for those in search of more than a mountain vacation. The place also offered special programs designed to heal broken hearts and strengthen connections. A great goal Susanna admired, of course, even though she seriously doubted it would have ever helped her family as her parents couldn't afford to take time off work for a vacation.

Hollie swept aside a branch, launching a shower of yellow and orange leaves. "I'm thankful for your help. When Ivy first came to live with us, her school records were scant since her parents died right before she started kindergarten."

"You and Jacob are doing an amazing job." She wasn't a parent, but after observing hundreds of parenting styles, she could see the trends of what worked and what didn't. "And it can't be easy adopting four children at once."

Hollie nodded as wind crooned through the clearing. "It isn't. Oh, and in case I forgot to say it. Thank you for the books on Dr. Dolittle. Elliot loved them."

The little boy had struggled with speaking since his biological parents died. He spoke only to animals at first. That was improving weekly, thank goodness. The book seemed a logical choice for the child processing such grief.

"I'm so glad he enjoyed them," she said. Atlas sniffed at a pile of sticks as they continued to navigate the well-marked trail, taking in the warm colors of the fall trees.

"You've got a real talent with the children. Your help, the help of all our friends here... I don't know how we would have managed the adoption process without our friends like you. Micah—Benji's dad—on the other hand, is alone."

"Do you mean that Micah's a single dad? Or that Benji's adopted?" Susanna closed her mouth fast to stem further questions. Benji Fuller was her student, and she didn't gossip. When she'd met Micah Fuller at the school orientation, she'd assumed he was Benji's father, and the man hadn't cleared up the misunderstanding. Of course, she'd only seen him briefly as he stopped by the library with Benji on their way to the class.

"Adopted," Hollie answered. "Well, almost. While Micah does have legal custody of Benji, the adoption is still being finalized. We met in the adoption support classes. Micah is actually Benji's uncle, same surname."

Although Susanna didn't gossip, she wasn't against listening, especially to a trusted source. So she simply answered with a "Hmm" as she paused for Atlas to "water" a signpost, then proceed back on the trail.

And while she understood that Micah Fuller might be going through some hurdles if he was new to the adoption process like Hollie, that didn't excuse the way he ignored her messages. If anything, he should be all the more concerned about his nephew. At the very least, he could have provided the boy's history to his school so they could best meet his needs. And she would tell him as much—politely—once she found him.

Meanwhile, she could still use this time to talk with Hollie about her children. "Okay, um, about Ivy, we're launching a parent-child story hour next week, with flexible days and times so working parents have the opportunity to come as well."

Hollie pressed a hand to her chest. "Thank goodness. I want to do right by my children, but we are also swamped here at Top Dog. I would hate to miss out on something because I overlooked a memo."

They'd already opened a second ranch location and were expanding their home base—the reason for all the construction that brought in Micah Fuller. Susanna just hoped it didn't steal the community feel from their small town that she'd come to love since moving here just over a year ago. The deafening sounds of the construction crew sure broke the peace of the wooded mountainside.

Stepping into the clearing, Susanna took in the breadth of work. The trees had been thinned to make spaces for campgrounds. It appeared they'd left the majority of the towering pines, and the wiring was being buried underground, camper hook-ups being hidden in mock birdhouses.

She'd wondered how this would still fit into the beauty of the ranch's architectural footprint, one that protected the integrity of the scenery. While the rest of the ranch sported a lodge and cabins, this would offer more accessibility to people on a budget, whether in a tent or campers.

And to professionals at "glamping."

While Susanna took in the construction work, Hollie knelt to give Atlas a scratch behind his furry ears. "Elliot talks about this little guy every day after school."

Her scrappy little black-and-white pup wagged his tail faster. Atlas had stolen her heart at first wag.

"He's my own little Top Dog." She'd gotten the idea to add Atlas to the library when she'd occasionally brought in one of the ranch's pups. Susanna had been hooked on the difference it made for the students. So much so, she'd promptly researched the proper channels to bring her personal pet to work on a regular basis.

Smiling, Hollie stood and called out to the construction crew scattered around the site. "Hello? Mr. Fuller? Has anyone seen Mr. Fuller?"

A pair of workmen loading brush into a truck stopped and pointed toward an excavator—thanks to hours reading to kindergarteners about trucks, Susanna could name every different one on this work site.

Still, she hadn't expected the owner of the company to be so hands-on, down to driving the equipment. She'd expected more of a clipboard sort of dude. An office guy who looked like he didn't lift anything heavier than his coffee and briefcase.

The night of the school open house he'd shown up in jeans and a polo shirt. She assumed he'd changed out of his work suit into more casual clothes. Now she realized he'd actually dressed up for the event.

Micah Fuller definitely wasn't a suit-wearing, pencil-pushing type today. Not even a polo-shirt-wearing type.

As she took in the hard-muscled man who could have doubled as a lumberjack, she knew he wasn't her type. But wow, he made her consider broadening her horizons.

Her breath hitched in her chest and her heart raced. He swung out from behind the controls of the excavator and his long-legged stride ate up the space between them. Well-worn denim encased hard-muscled thighs, his jeans low slung on slim hips.

She swallowed in a slow gulp before letting her gaze travel upward to his…yep…broad shoulders. The yellow construction vest was rather ironic since this man didn't need help drawing attention. He wasn't the kind to fade into the scenery, to be overlooked in the library while hunched over a book.

She hated the way insecurity crept up in spite of her best effort. A *Jane Eyre* quote floated through her brain. *Do you think, because I am poor, obscure, plain and little, I am soulless and heartless?*

You think wrong! She'd graduated top of her class in undergrad and graduate schools. Plain and little did not equate to less worthy, for crying out loud.

His hard hat shaded his face as he turned to speak to the man walking alongside him. After lots of pointing, he turned his full attention in her direction.

Once he stepped past the construction tape, he swept off his hat, his hair dark and close cropped. His eyes icy blue and piercing. How had she missed the boat so much that orientation day? There'd been a crowd, but that wasn't much of an excuse.

What surprised her most? He was younger than she recalled from their brief meeting. He couldn't be older than his early thirties. That young and he owned his own company? She was still struggling to make her college loan payments.

And just thinking about those loans reminded her of how hard she'd worked for her job. At the last school, she'd dated a parent only to have things turn tense—very tense—when they broke up. She'd moved to this position to leave all that negativity and tension behind.

No man—no matter how hot—would tempt her to risk this fresh start. Especially not one like

Micah Fuller who couldn't even be bothered to answer her messages about his new little charge.

Micah Fuller fought back irritation over the interruption.

He'd overslept, then stepped on a Lego. Benji insisted on wearing his favorite orange shirt—which had been hiding in the bottom of a basket of unfolded laundry. At least it was clean. Micah had pulled up to the school right as the bell had rung, so he'd had to go inside to sign Benji into the office for a late slip.

Work was usually Micah's haven. But no such luck today. Two of his crew called in sick and the backhoe was broken.

And now Hollie O'Brien—the lady who signed his paycheck—was here giving a tour to a pretty Tinker Bell of a woman and her tiny pooch.

Yeah, it was a banner day.

"Mrs. O'Brien, what can I help you with?" Micah hitched his hands in his back pockets.

Smiling, Hollie gestured to the lady beside her. "I'm just the navigator today, showing Miss Levine the way. And now that she's found you, I need to return this phone call."

Holding up her cell, Hollie backed away. Leaving him alone with the pixie in ankle boots, leggings and some kind of yarn poncho. She tightened her grip on her rhinestone-studded dog leash and thrust out her other hand. "I'm Susanna Levine from Moonlight Ridge Elementary and I'm here about Benji."

From the school?

Panic jackhammered his gut. "I sent the cupcakes for the party. I dropped them off in the office and I attached a note with Benji's name and class on top."

If some other kids had eaten those cupcakes, he was going to lose his mind. He'd stayed up until three in the morning baking them and was proud of the results. He wasn't the best at frosting, sure, but he'd covered up the torn bits with crushed chocolate cookies and gummy worms that he thought sort of looked like they were burrowing up out of dirt.

"I'm not here about cupcakes—"

"And I filled out the permission slip for his field trip. Do you need a chaperone?"

Holding his breath, he tried to deny the fear that clawed up his throat over the possibility of being stuck on a school bus with a class of first-graders.

She shook her head, her silky, brown hair sliding over her shoulder. "I'm not here about any of that. You haven't answered my messages."

Her polite tone didn't hide the hint of steely judgment in her brown eyes.

He pulled out his phone fast to check for missed calls. "I'm not sure I understand since you're not his teacher. Is Benji hurt? Are you the school nurse?"

"I'm Susanna Levine," she repeated slowly, louder this time, a tic twitching in the corner of her eye. "The librarian. Benji is fine. I've sent text messages and even put notes in Benji's planner for over a week and haven't heard back from you. I need to set up a time to talk about Benji's reading."

He snapped his fingers. "The librarian. Ah, now I remember you from the open house." Tucking the phone back in his pocket, he crossed his arms. "I'm listening."

"Preferably somewhere quieter," she shouted even louder, scooping up her fur ball of a dog.

Sighing, he shot a glance at his crew. As long as he could keep them in sight. He texted a quick set of instructions to the foreman, then tucked his cell into his back pocket.

"Alright, ma'am. Let's go over to that picnic table. I've got fifteen minutes." He charged ahead, dusting leaves and pine needles off the planked seat. Then he motioned for her to sit before taking his place across from her. "What's going on with Benji?"

Her eyebrows lifted at his brusque manner, but he didn't have time for niceties. He needed her to get to the point so he could get back to work. He needed this job to put his business on the map. The stakes were higher than ever now that he was responsible for his nephew.

"Well." She placed her dog back on the ground and looped the leash around her hand. "Benji's reading isn't up to grade level. It's not even close."

Something that felt a lot like defeat settled on his shoulders. This was the last thing he'd expected to hear and the thing he felt least equipped to help with. His experience with kids was limited to the past four months with Benji.

Micah's brother and sister-in-law had been drug addicts, unable to care for their child. His parents had tried, but they ultimately decided they were too old to take on bringing up a grandchild. Micah just wished they'd all figured it out sooner so he could have stepped in earlier and Benji could have had less upheaval in his young life.

He was determined not to fail his nephew…soon to be legally his son. And yeah, he loved the kid every bit as much as any child he would have had even if Benji still called him Uncle Micah.

Scrubbing a hand over his stubbled jaw, he searched the librarian's face. They'd gotten off to a rocky start and he needed her as his ally. "What does his teacher have to say about that?"

"I'm the reading specialist. Mrs. Yoder has reached out to you as well but hasn't heard back either. I prefer to think we simply have the wrong number and not that you're disinterested."

He couldn't decide whether to be angry at the dressing-down or amused at her assertive tactics.

"I'm not disinterested," he assured her.

"Alright, then. Just to be clear, is this your phone number?" She held up her cell for him to check the screen.

He shook his head. "That's my parents' number." And the fact that they hadn't bothered to notify him had him grinding his teeth. "I check Benji's planner daily. I haven't seen any notes."

"Fair enough. I apologize." Her face softened into a smile. "I trust, though, that you'll understand why I decided to take a more direct route and set up a time for you to meet with both of us." She tucked a strand of her bouncy, shoulder-length hair behind her ear. The wind almost gusted, turning her pale cheeks as rosy as her lips.

Clearing his throat, he tore away his gaze. "Then I'll give you my current cell number—"

Her jaw jutted. "Regardless, I'm not leaving any more messages."

"Listen, this was just a mix-up." Frustration was fast overtaking any possible humor, even if it didn't dampen the wayward attraction. "I appreciate your care for Benji. I really do. But I need you to know I'm trying harder than anyone for my boy."

"No, sir, you're not," she said in a quiet voice that undoubtedly held the power to shush even a library full of rowdy children. "Benji's trying harder than anyone."

That cut. Deep. He needed to check his ego because, yes, he could concede that point. "Tell me what I need to do."

"I'm leading a parent enrichment session on powering up your child's reading at home."

"When is it?" Please, he hoped it wasn't during work hours. He already hated that Benji had to go to day care after school. At least he was able to make use of the ranch's sitter service for the children of staff and guests. He could extend a couple of hours for Benji to stay, but they already spent too much time apart and Benji still cried at the morning drop-off. He tried to hide it, but just this morning, Micah saw the tears sheening before the boy swiped his sleeve across his face.

He would do anything for Benji. Anything.

"Six o'clock tomorrow evening. It's fine to bring Benji along." She fished into her massive bag, pulled out a packet of papers and slid them across the table. "And it would be helpful if you could fill out these before you come. I also sent them to you in an email."

Thumbing the thick yellow envelope that felt more like a small book, he already saw another late night in his future.

"Should I bake cupcakes?" he asked dryly.

"That would be awesome," she said pertly, snapping her fingers for her dog to join her. "See you tomorrow, Mr. Fuller."

As he watched the twitch of her hips and glide of her hair as she picked her way around a trailer full of lumber, he knew he didn't have time to date.

He didn't even really have time for a fling, particularly not with one of Benji's teachers.

Still, he couldn't help but wonder what cupcake flavor was her favorite.

Chapter Two

Turning the page on *The Paper Bag Princess*, Susanna plastered a smile on her face as she led story time with kids and the parents. Inside, though, she was irked and frustrated.

Micah Fuller still hadn't shown up with Benji at the school library tonight. Hadn't he promised to be here just yesterday when she'd told him about the reading enrichment meeting? Her workdays were long enough without making special trips to track down parents who didn't respond when contacted through regular channels. Sure, people had emergencies. But she'd given him the benefit of the doubt once, and now this was starting to look like a pattern.

Encouraging interaction from the kids, she perched on a stool and poured her focus into the storytelling with Atlas curled up asleep on her feet. Children sat on the rug around her, the pastel fantasy pattern matching the murals she'd painted on the walls.

When she'd started this job last year, the walls had been stark white. Clinical. Lifeless. With no imagination. She'd always dabbled in art—it had been her minor in undergrad.

As soon as she'd signed her contract with Moonlight Ridge Elementary, Susanna spent a few months learning all she could about the area. So many myths, so many nearly magical encounters with animals. When it came time to make this space more inviting, Susanna had painted sprawling mountains, a twilight sky and a green dragon with a stag on the ridgeline.

Today, the students wore assorted puppets that they waved throughout the story. Interaction with texts helped with retention and comprehension, something she would discuss in more detail with the adults shortly.

Parents stood behind the kids. She'd opted to

read a book first to give latecomers an opportunity to straggle in. But she was fast approaching the last page.

"The end," she announced, placing the book beside her. "So let's talk about the story for a moment. In this book, the characters had different jobs. Just like people have jobs, dogs have jobs too. What do you think some of those jobs might be?"

Answers echoed from the children sitting crisscross applesauce on the rug.

Curtis, one of the more vocal students in the group and almost always first to chime in, tapped his fingers to his face. His green eyes lit up as he spoke. "The kind of dog with spots, for a firehouse."

"Police dogs," Curtis's best friend chimed in, not to be outdone by his popular buddy.

His answer unleashed a flood of responses fired too quickly to tell where they came from.

"Service dogs."

"Guide dogs."

"And the ones that search for missing kids."

"Exactly," Susanna agreed, cracking her toes in her canvas shoes, her feet aching. It seemed like a lifetime ago that she'd put on the maxi jean dress and sweater. "Who can tell the grown-ups what kind of job Atlas has?"

"Me, me," Benji's voice blasted from the door as he rushed in, breathless. His blond hair was wind-ruffled, his sweatshirt printed with a Top Dog Dude Ranch logo. "Atlas is a therapy dog who makes us feel better when we read."

Micah trailed in after the boy, holding a plastic container. The promised baked goods? Her heart softened just a touch over his tardiness.

And her breath hitched at the sight of his shoulders in the leather jacket.

She pulled her gaze off the hot single dad and back onto her student. "That's right, Benji. And you're just in time to join the other children for craft and movie time. So if everyone will stand and follow Ivy's mom…"

Hollie O'Brien peeled away from the other parents and motioned for the dozen kids to join her as she opened the door to the media room that had an observation window so parents could still see their children. "This way. I have all sorts of fun crafts from the ranch for everyone."

Standing, Susanna clapped her hands together and announced, "Parents, thank you for coming out tonight. Once you've all gotten a snack and taken a seat, we'll get started."

Micah angled through the press of people and set the container on the table beside her. "I know I promised cupcakes. But Benji asked to make cookies. I was careful about no peanuts and no raisins. Sugar cookies so Benji could help with the frosting and sprinkles. I've learned that kids love lots of sprinkles."

He stood so close she could smell the leather of his jacket and the musk of his aftershave. A shiver tingled up her spine.

Hauling her gaze away, she peeked in the corner and saw adorably messy cookies with a hefty dousing of colorful sprinkles. She pulled one out and popped it into her mouth.

"That's good," she said with surprise. "Thank you. I didn't have supper yet."

She licked the frosting from the corner of her mouth, only to stop short as she caught his gaze lingering on her lips. Heat rushed through her, and she hoped it hadn't betrayed her by hitting her cheeks.

Clearing her throat, she set the rest of the cookie on a napkin. "Thank you. And thank you for coming here tonight. I recognize that my approach tracking you down at work was unconventional, but I assure you I have Benji's best interest at heart."

Atlas padded across the floor, circling around the legs of the table until his leash tugged tight. He strained to sniff along the hem of Micah's pant leg. Kneeling, she untangled her dog quickly, grateful for the moment to pull her attention off his vibrant blue eyes.

"Understood." He rocked back on his boot heels, the toes scuffed and well worn. "Sorry we're late. There was a crisis at work."

Letting the excuse slide, she shot a glance at the other parents and found them busily piling their plates with fruit, cheese and small cups of granola. She turned her attention back to Micah. "What did Benji have to say about our conversation yesterday?"

He scrubbed a hand along his five-o'clock shadow. "I didn't say anything to him about our talk."

"Um, okay." Toying with the braided leash, she pressed her lips into a tight line to keep from blurting out words she might regret later. She wasn't normally impulsive but something about this man left her off balance.

Atlas pulled toward Micah again and she knelt to scoop the pup up just as Micah bent to smooth a hand along the dog's spine. Atlas panted, leaning into the petting, his tail wagging furiously.

Her gaze met his for an instant and held, sending a tingle along her spine. Clearing her throat, she stood, cradling Atlas and stealing some of his comfort for herself. Micah rose as well, unfolding his big muscular body.

"I don't have a lot of experience with kids. But I thought I should wait to see what this meeting held." He scratched the back of his head with a sheepish wince. "I didn't want to do the wrong thing and make him feel insecure or worry that he's in trouble. I wanted to come to this meeting first to gather info for the game plan."

Thump. Thump. Thump. Atlas's tail wagged, swatting her arm. Micah smiled down at the pup, and Susanna tried not to notice how he looked a bit like a modern-day knight in his leather jacket and scruff—especially with the painted green dragon peaking over his shoulder.

"That's insightful," she conceded. "Information is powerful. I would also suggest that you not let your worries paralyze you. If you listen to Benji, just listen, you don't have to solve everything that moment. Hearing his perspective is just as valuable as any dry research."

"I'm not even close to father-of-the-year material, but I'm all Benji has." He reached into his leather jacket and pulled out the manila envelope full of papers. His face creased into a smile that pushed surprising dimples into his cheeks. "All filled out. I'm ready to be schooled."

Benji hated school. And he really hated reading.

But he liked Miss Levine and Atlas, which was a problem. Because he couldn't read. Not much, anyway. So it was hard not to raise his hand and answer.

Scooping up a juice box, he stabbed the straw in. He took his time sipping as he looked around at the other kids. How long would this meeting last? His stomach knotted with nerves.

Would people be talking about him at school tomorrow?

He could say his ABCs, and he could tell the teacher what sound each letter made. He just couldn't put them together into words when he looked at them on the page. The parts of the sentence jumped around in front of his eyes. He'd gotten better at guessing, based on figuring out one or two of the letters and looking at the pictures.

It was slow, though. So slow, people like Curtis laughed.

He missed his old school, back when they didn't care about reading. It was all crafts and playing outside.

Here, his only friend in class was a girl. Ivy O'Brien was okay. For a girl. But hearing her read made him feel even worse. She was smarter than all the kids and he was a real—

"Hey, dummy," Curtis called out. "The baby books are over there."

The two boys beside Curtis laughed. Curtis had lots of friends.

"Curtis," Mrs. O'Brien said softly, "we don't call each other names. That's rude. Do you understand?"

"Yes, ma'am," Curtis said, hanging his head in a fakey-sad way.

"Now, you need to apologize," Mrs. O'Brien urged.

Ugh. No. Benji's face went hot.

"I'm sorry, Benji." Curtis held his hand out to shake, his back to Mrs. O'Brien as he whispered, "Big dummy."

Benji wanted to shout back at Curtis. But that would only make everybody look at him. And the last thing he needed was to have to repeat what Curtis said. Curtis would probably lie anyway.

So, Benji turned and pitched his juice box into the trash can. Apple juice splattered upward.

Waving, Ivy called, "Come over here. The movie's about to start."

Shuffling across the rug with the solar system on it, he sat beside her, right on top of Mars, the red planet. He loved hearing about the planets and outer space. "Are you sure you wanna be seen with a dummy?"

"Don't listen to him." She tipped her bucket of popcorn for him to see inside and whispered, "Have some. It's got fairy dust."

He peered in and saw sprinkles and candy mixed in.

"Thanks," he whispered back, stuffing a handful into his mouth.

"I've wanted to watch this all day. I loved, loved, loved the book."

The book? He stifled a wince and picked out the green candies, his favorite. Crunching, he reminded himself since Ivy was here, too, this meeting wasn't just for kids who were having trouble in school. Maybe it really was just about meeting the parents and passing out lists of good books to read. He had to do everything he could to hide how hard it was for him to figure out words.

Because if Uncle Micah figured out he was adopting a dummy, he might dump him too.

Micah couldn't recall a week where he'd been this worn out on a Friday. He put the truck in Park outside the log cabin, porch light shining down on pumpkins and bales of hay that decorated their porch—compliments of the Top Dog Dude Ranch.

Getting to stay in a two-bedroom cabin at the ranch was a perk from this job. Benji got to participate in all the vacation activities provided for guests. And he'd made friends with some of the staff's families—like Hollie and Jacob O'Brien's four children and the triplets whose mom ran the gift shop.

Triplets. The word made him shudder. He was barely keeping his head above water with one kid.

At least he'd finished the week armed with more info on how to help Benji with his homework. An entire binder full of information on reading enrichment.

He was definitely out of his depth, but still trying. That's all he could do.

"You ready back there, partner?" He looked up at the rearview mirror and saw Benji jolt awake, blue eyes blinking to adjust to the subdued glow from the porch light.

The boy swept his sleeve across his mouth to wipe away drool. "Uh-huh."

"Do you want me to carry you?"

He shook his head, grabbed his book bag and unbuckled his booster seat. "I don't wanna go to bed yet. I'm really, really hungry."

"I'll see what I can rustle up." He opened the back door of the extended cab and lifted Benji out. The boy's backpack dragged through the dirt, then thumped up the cabin steps, but Benji had it in such a death grip, Micah decided not to press the point. His nephew insisted on being independent and Micah tried to support those efforts whenever possible to build the boy's confidence.

At least that's what he'd read online when researching this parenting gig.

Inside the cabin, he turned on the lights, reflecting warmth off the pine of the cabin walls. Before Benji, Micah's living room and kitchen had been bare-bones—a massive recliner, a wide-screen television, a lonely coffeepot on the counter.

Now? He still couldn't get over the changes. Toy construction trucks were parked underneath the bar stools. A blanket featuring Benji's favorite superhero was strewn across the back of the blue sofa.

Micah pulled out a loaf of bread, peanut butter and strawberry preserves from the Top Dog diner. He needed to go into town to the grocery store, but hadn't been able to find the time. He cut the crust off the bread the way the kid liked. He still didn't have the skill down to a science yet, parts of the bread tearing. But by the time he made an extra sandwich there was enough to call it a full one.

He poured a cup of milk for Benji and a second for himself. He needed to look into cooking classes. How long could a kid live off meals of PBJs, cereal and nuggets?

Oh, and cookies.

But the last thing he needed was to think of the smile of approval as Susanna Levine had inspected his baked goods. Or the bliss on her face as she bit into one and licked the frosting off her plump lip.

And she didn't even know how hard he'd worked to make them.

The kitchen was a disaster from cookie prep and breakfast. An art project from school—a paper plate pumpkin—was anchored to the refrigerator with a magnet. He was trying his best, but words from Susanna Levine echoed through his mind. How she'd encouraged him to broach the subject with Benji—and listen.

Micah set the paper plate with the sandwich on the island with a small glass of milk. "Benji, I got a visit yesterday from the librarian at your school."

"Miss Levine?" He clambered up onto the bar stool. "She's really nice. Is that why we went to the special story hour tonight?"

"Yes, she told me about it." He tapped his thumb along his own glass of milk. "Why didn't you give me the messages from her? She said they were in your planner."

"You didn't ask to see it on Friday." He tore at his sandwich, his blue eyes downcast and wary. "That's where the messages are."

Micah bit back the urge to call him on the evasion. This wasn't the time to teach him a lesson about quibbling, and he didn't want Benji to shut down. "I know I'm the grown-up and I should remember those things. But I'm going to need your help getting into the routine of school. Okay? And if your teachers ask to speak to me, I need to know that."

And how did he feel about spending more time with the distracting librarian? He wasn't sure of anything except that Benji needed his full focus during this crucial time of transition.

Benji turned his plate around and around on the butcher-block counter, his jaw trembling. "I was scared you were gonna get mad at me for getting bad grades."

The words sucker punched him right in the heart.

"Hey, hey, buddy," he said softly, patting Benji on the back. "You haven't done anything wrong."

"But I'm getting bad grades," he repeated in a wobbly voice, his little shoulders sagging. "I'm trying hard, I really am. I'll pick up my toys. Whatever you say."

Micah could hear the unspoken fear of rejection in the boy's voice, a tone that had really ramped up after Benji's grandparents had declared they were in over their heads. His mind echoed with Susanna's words about how hard Benji was trying. Micah knew too well how deeply his parents' disappointment could cut.

Sighing, he sat on the other bar stool beside

him. "Miss Levine says you're working really hard." He weighed his words, hoping he wasn't making things worse. He was still so new at this parenting gig. "The grades just tell us what we need to do to help you as you learn."

Benji's forehead creased as he pondered for a moment. He squeezed the sandwich between his fingertips. The soft bread squished, the jelly pooling slightly from the edge and onto the paper plate. Benji swiped a finger across the oozing jelly before licking it off.

Finally, the boy let out a deep sigh, his eyes meeting Micah's. "Atlas really helps me read at school. I like telling stories to him."

"That's what Miss Levine told me too." The dog had been a real icebreaker for the parents tonight too.

"When I got to sit on the mat with Atlas, I finished three books in story time at the library this week." He stuffed a PBJ quarter in his mouth.

"We'll have to celebrate with ice cream this weekend. With sprinkles." That counted as milk, right? "After supper, of course."

"Um, okay." He scuffed the toe of his sneakers along a rung on the bar stool.

"Is there something else you would prefer?"

He almost offered cookies, then remembered he should back off the sugar and he'd already brought up ice cream. "What about extra time tossing the ball around? Or we could go fishing this weekend? Even a pony ride, perhaps?"

"Those sound okay." He chewed his bottom lip for a moment before continuing, "But there is something I really, really want."

"Just name it. If I can make it happen, I will."

He swiped his mouth with the hem of his sweatshirt, excitement chasing away the dejected look in his eyes. "Oh, you can make it happen."

Man, the kid had a smile that could charm apples off the trees. Every sacrifice he was making was 100 percent worth it. He pushed aside thoughts of Susanna and focused on his nephew. "Are you going to tell me what it is or do I need to keep guessing?"

Benji's double-bright smile offered only a hint of warning. "I want a puppy. A puppy of my own."

Great. Micah bit back a sigh and drained his glass of milk. The last thing he needed was another living being to take care of. He could barely manage as it was. But the kid had already lost so many people who claimed to love him. His parents had chosen drugs over their son. Benji had even lost his home. If he wanted the moon, Micah intended to begin building a ladder.

"Sure, kiddo. We'll start looking for a puppy."

"Cool! Thank you." Benji hugged him hard before plopping back onto the bar stool. "Can we invite Atlas and Miss Levine over for a playdate?"

Chapter Three

Susanna hadn't taken much time for play in her life. She'd always been focused on school and not drawing attention to herself. Her parents had worked so many hours to keep food on the table, she'd had to learn how to organize a rigorous schedule by herself, with minimal support at home. She'd gone to college on a partial scholarship, working two part-time jobs.

Since moving to Moonlight Ridge, she'd "played" more than in her whole twenty-eight years.

She'd also found friends along the way—and

healing too. This was her place. These were her people.

Hopefully, today's animal rescue fundraiser at the ranch would bring healing to others as well. She needed to focus on that and ignore distractions, like an attraction to Micah Fuller.

Clipboard in hand, she logged in donations for a local animal rescue and passed out donation receipts. Bags were being slung into the back of one of the ranch's trucks. Bins around her overflowed with toys and blankets. Barking echoed from one of the barns hosting the shelter's adopt-a-thon with cats, dogs and even two horses. A mobile vaccination van was set up beside the barn, a line of pet owners snaking all the way to the tree line, some with dogs on leashes, others with pets in carriers.

She'd always loved animals and believed in the animal rescue mission. But after adopting Atlas, the cause had taken on a deeper, more personal meaning.

The ranch's band—Raise the Woof—played on the back of a wagon. Banjo chords mingled with conversation and rich laughter and Susanna's boots stirred loose gravel. She carefully weaved around the bales of hay, cornstalks and pumpkins littered around the sound equipment. The pickup band was composed of staff from the ranch.

Some faces she recognized, like the new stable manager, Eliza Hubbard, playing keyboards. And the landscaper, Charlotte Pace, was singing backup vocals. The audience included a mixture of ranch guests and members of the community, applauding as the song ended. Even the sheriff was clapping along to the beat off to the side.

Closing out with a musical flourish, the band took a bow. Eliza leaned into her mic, side ponytail draping over her shoulder. "We're going to break for five. But we hope you'll stick around for a message from our amazing bosses—Hollie and Jacob O'Brien."

The husband and wife leaped up onto the wagon, each taking a microphone. Hollie stood by her husband in matching blue flannel shirts and jean jackets, hers with rhinestones.

Jacob tipped his tan Stetson to the crowd. "Welcome to Moonlight Ridge, Tennessee, home to the Top Dog Dude Ranch, renowned for family-friendly rustic retreats that bring people together and heal broken hearts. Some say it's the majestic mountain vistas. Others vow there's magic in the hot springs. But all agree there's something special about the four-legged creatures at the Top Dog Dude Ranch here that give our guests a 'new leash on love.'"

Smiling wide, Hollie gestured to the crowd with one hand as she lifted her mic with the other. "It takes a village to make the magic, and we would like to introduce you to a couple of those people who—while they aren't a part of our staff—we consider them Top Dog family. Sheriff Declan Winslow—" she pointed toward the rangy law enforcement officer standing under a gnarled oak tree whose leaves were riotous shades of reds and oranges "—keeps our area safe, going above and beyond. He's here on his day off."

Applause rippled through the crowd.

Once it quieted, Hollie continued, gesturing Susanna's way. "And Susanna Levine, the librarian at our elementary school. She and Atlas are wonderful ambassadors for the wonders of pet therapy. Miss Levine, with help from Atlas, will be conducting a story time over by the adoption event."

Face burning, Susanna brushed aside the praise with a shake of the head and a dismissive, embarrassed hand wave. She knew she was good at her job. She knew it was her calling. But this level of attention always left her uneasy. Tightening her grip on the clipboard, she managed a smile while thinking that all the attention should be on the animals in need of support.

Atlas was currently chilling out in the O'Briens' office, resting up from all the snuggles and attention of the morning story time, resting up before the next round scheduled for later in the afternoon. As Hollie and Jacob continued their welcoming intro, Susanna felt a hand on her shoulder. She turned, surprised to find the stable manager, Eliza. Her cowgirl hat cast shadows over her pale face. The stable manager gave a grin, her green eyes a perfect contrast to the purple plaid button-up shirt and jeans.

"Hi there, Eliza," Susanna said, passing over the clipboard to a shelter volunteer, then easing back from the crowd so as not to disturb the announcements. "I didn't know you play the keyboards. Nice job. You're a woman of many talents."

Laughing, Eliza picked a stray piece of pale hay off her shirt. "I don't know about talent, but my mother sure had me practice long enough as a child that I can hammer through the melody."

"The turnout is incredible." Susanna scanned the dense crowd that had resumed its churning chatter. No matter how much time passed since the pandemic's end, it was still surreal to be gathering like this again. A gift she didn't take for granted. The sound of laughter from all ages filled the air, all ages. Her gaze landed on Benji playing with the O'Brien children and triplet boys. She couldn't stop herself from searching for Micah. "This place has sure made quite a name as the place to heal."

Chuckling, Eliza winced. "No pressure."

"You're not fooling me. It's clear you love your job."

"Well, getting to lead trail rides is a definite dream come true. But there's more to my job and this place. What's not to love about goat yoga with a family reunion? Bonfires and zip-lining with a youth group?" She tipped back her hat, shooting a smile and a wink. "Or couples making essential oils to use during massages."

Had it really been two years since she'd indulged in anything that resulted in a man's hands on her body, soothing away the aches of the day?

"Certainly sounds romantic," Susanna said, taking in a breath of fresh air and smelling homemade pumpkin pie. Her mouth watered and her stomach involuntary grumbled softly. "And of course, the hot springs and its amazing legend. We need more retreats like this."

Eliza scuffed her worn boots through the dirt. "I appreciate that you were able to come over to do story time with Atlas. I know the call was last-minute, but we had an employee call in sick, which left us with holes in the schedule."

"I was planning to come help with the food drive, so it wasn't any trouble to lead a couple of story groups. The Top Dog Dude Ranch is an integral part of the community. I may be new here, but I intend to put down roots." She'd never had a place to call home for any length of time. She'd chosen this place with care and intended to cultivate the connection.

"What did you think of Micah Fuller?"

The question caught her by surprise. She blinked, trying to get her bearings.

Why was Eliza asking that? Then Susanna remembered that Eliza had pointed her toward Hollie during the search for Micah earlier in the week. "I think he's trying his best to step up with his nephew."

"Trying, huh?" Eliza grimaced. "That's not a rousing endorsement."

"He's the father of a student. So I don't have much more to say." She grasped the convenient copout to evade the question.

"Ah, is that interest I detect in your voice?"

Interest? No. Attraction? Well, that was another matter and far more complicated, as she knew all too well. And for that reason, she needed to shut down this line of discussion fast.

The last thing she wanted was to dredge all of that up again. How she'd fallen for a guy, only to find out his daughter went to her school. Back then, Susanna was purely a reading specialist at a private school—and little Rosalee had been one of her students.

Things had gotten so complicated and stressful after the breakup. Sure, a significant factor in that came from the fact that Rosalee's grandparents were major donors to the academy.

Legally, the school had no cause to let her go. And she probably could have weathered the storm. But it was easier to look for a job elsewhere. She hated that she'd caved. Hated her avoidance of conflict.

And she was working on that flaw in her character, but it was tough to break a lifetime habit of keeping her head down and plowing through to get a job done. Meanwhile, though, she didn't intend to do anything that would jeopardize this second chance at a pocket of peace she'd found in this beautiful community. "Not interested. Really not interested. And even if I was, his little boy is one of my students. So, in case you were wondering, I'm completely okay if *you* want to check out Micah."

Eliza rolled her eyes. "He's probably ten years younger than I am. But thanks for the compliment. And nice try diverting me. A significant portion of Moonlight Ridge has a child, stepchild, niece, nephew or grandchild at your school. How are you supposed to find anyone to date?"

There were a lot of *ifs* that would be needed to get her to that point after how badly she'd been burned.

"I'm too busy working to pay off school loans to think about anything else." She massaged a hand along her collarbone to ease the constriction in her chest. In her mind's eye, the outstanding balance blinking on the computer screen flashed before her eyes. Sometimes it felt impossible to get out from under the sacrifices she had made to pursue her calling. Susanna did her best impression of a put-together smile.

"I can understand needing to put your career first." Eliza nodded, before continuing. "Then you won't have a problem with the fact that he's due here any minute to pick out a—"

"Puppy, puppy, puppy," Benji called out, his words as fast as his feet pounding the earth, high stepping over pumpkins toward her. "Miss Levine, Uncle Micah said I could have a puppy to help me with my reading. Like Atlas."

The little boy screeched to a halt in front of her, his blue eyes sparkling with excitement.

"Wow, that's awesome." Although she wondered who was going to train the puppy when the guy could barely keep up with the demands of parenting. And more importantly, why was she scanning the crowd looking for his broad shoulders? "Where is your uncle, sweetie? We don't want him to worry about you."

Benji pointed over his shoulder. "He's right behind me. See?"

Sure enough, he was maybe twenty yards away, the breeze ruffling his wavy, black hair. His hands were stuffed in the pockets of his hoodie sweatshirt as he wove around pumpkins on his way over. The sun shone down on the handsome hard angles of his face, his square jaw all but calling to her hand to test the stubble.

And the confidence in his bold strides? Pure magnetism.

Eliza's gaze skipped from her to Micah and back again with a little too much intuitiveness. The stable manager rested a hand on Benji's shoulder. "Hello there, kiddo."

"Hi, Miss Hubbard. I'm going to see the puppies. Come on." He grabbed her hand and tugged. Hard.

"Hang on, kiddo," she exclaimed, laughing, stumbling after him. "Susanna, let Micah know where we are. Okay?"

Before Susanna could issue a resounding "no" and backpedal away, Eliza was making fast tracks toward the barn with the enthusiastic boy hauling her by the hand.

Leaving Susanna directly in the path of the boy's too-hot uncle.

Since he prided himself on being able to work alongside his employees every step of the way, Micah wondered how a six-year-old could leave him in the dust.

And to make matters worse, the librarian was witness to his ineptitude.

Did she have to look so smug and cute in her

light-up pumpkin necklace, sweatshirt and leggings? How she made fuzzy boots look hot was beyond him. He'd heard her voice carrying on the wind, talking about school loans and then chatting with Benji. Except he hadn't caught what they said.

The simple sound of a woman's voice shouldn't have him so distracted.

"Good afternoon." He stopped alongside her, drawn to the warmth of her brown eyes. "Did you happen to see my kid come blasting through this way?"

A quick nod sent her brunette hair rippling. "Benji just went with Eliza Hubbard—the stable manager—to the barn where they're holding the adoption event."

She pointed across the sea of people to where Benji stood at the barn doors holding the stable manager's hand as they looked into a pen of puppies.

He breathed a sigh of relief. "I didn't expect to see you here."

"I'm just helping out my friend Hollie." She toyed with the pumpkin necklace, plastic pumpkins flashing.

Nervous?

Interesting. He should walk away. Should. But

didn't. Instead, he leaned against the split rail fence. Beyond in the pasture, a cream-colored horse began to wander toward them. "We're here because Benji wants a puppy. I heard about the adoption event."

"Benji told me." She nodded toward the child cuddling a big fluffy pup and sitting on a bale of hay. Next to the child and dog, pumpkins and gourds gathered against the fence. The puppy leaped from the arms of the child, sniffing at the display. "Puppies are a lot of work."

Did she know how cute she was when she put on that uptight air? "Do I detect a note of judgment in your tone?"

She crossed her arms defensively. "Just concerned about how the puppy will get the attention it needs while Benji's at school and you're at work."

Still, it irked him that she might think he had screwed up on this too. "The ranch has a doggy day care. I plan for the puppy to go there."

"But it can't go until it's had all of the vaccines," she pointed out just as the horse reached the split rail fence. He chuffed, nudging Susanna's free hand. She let the mare smell her palm before she continued. "That can take weeks, or even months, depending on how many, if any, the pup has had."

She had him there. He was curious, though, why she was working so hard to deter him.

"Until he can get those shots, I'll check in on my lunch break and hire a dog walker too."

"I shouldn't have spoken. It's not my place."

True enough. But he was still curious about why she had it out for him. "Share what you're thinking. I won't bite."

Her eyebrows lifted for a moment before she responded. "Okay, since you asked. I don't want Benji to be disappointed in his puppy. Pet therapy isn't that simple. The dog doesn't know what to do from the start."

"That's a valid point and luckily for me and for Benji, I can check in with you on all those steps. But you told me to follow my instincts, and this is the first time Benji has made a request. I plan to honor it." He held up his palm to let the horse sniff him before he moved to stroke the animal's velvety-soft neck. The horse leaned into the touch, stretching.

"Alright. Whatever I can do to help, I'm in. Starting now, I recommend you reach out to the Top Dog's stable manager. Eliza Hubbard has her degree in some sort of animal-assisted therapy.

I only got Atlas recently. Before that I read with dogs from the ranch."

Was she really trying to pawn him off onto someone else? He wasn't that easily deterred. She'd wanted his attention? Well, he'd listened.

"Why did you wait to get a dog of your own?"

"Lots of reasons, actually. I believe that a pet is a big financial commitment, a decision that shouldn't be made impulsively. I needed to save up after my move." She scrunched her nose. "You may have guessed that a school librarian with a mountain of college debt wouldn't be rolling in cash."

Her arms crossed tight over her chest drew his eyes to her subtle curves. Clearing his throat and drawing his eyes respectfully back to her face.

"Fair enough. I'll take your tips about pet ownership under advisement." He should walk away. Really should. He'd obviously hit some buttons with her, and she was giving him warning signals left and right not to push further. But Benji was playing so nicely with the puppies under the watchful eye of ranch staff, and he couldn't remember when he'd enjoyed sparring with a woman this much. He didn't want to say goodbye. Not yet. "I don't know how I'll ever be able to thank you for all you've already done for us."

"You thanked me before. And I appreciate it. But this is my job and I love it." A wry grin spread across her face. "So much so that I took out college loans to pay for a degree that will never make me rich."

"I realize it's your job, but I also know I need a lot more guidance than most of the other parents." An idea started to take root in his mind. "And I'm not afraid to ask for help. I can't handle it all and I'm not too proud to admit it."

Her face softened, some of the defensiveness leaving her shoulders. "I can give you additional resources based on what his testing says."

"I'm not talking about more websites or handouts." The more he spoke, the more the idea felt right. Just like when he made a business decision. Trust the instincts. Full steam ahead. "Regardless of the diagnosis, it's clear he needs one-on-one assistance."

"That would certainly help and I'm glad you're open to that option." Her brown eyes filled with compassion. "Many parents either don't want to admit they need help or can't afford the cost. The school has a list of tutors who come highly recommended."

"I'm sure they're top-notch," he acknowledged even as he also knew he wasn't letting her off the hook so easily. Benji's well-being was too important. Life had dealt the child second best too many times. For better or worse, Micah was the boy's only advocate. "But you're also top-notch, and Benji already trusts you."

"He's a great kid." Her eyes shifted toward where Benji was romping around with a puppy under the watchful supervision of the stable manager. Benji clapped his hands, whooping with the pup. "I'm sure he will develop a relationship with whoever you choose to be his tutor."

Benji might look like a regular, easygoing boy right now, but Micah knew all too well the loss, the trauma the boy had suffered.

"See, that's the problem. Benji bonds slowly." True. Heartbreakingly so if he let himself think about it too much. "And I want to make sure he's on track before we move."

"Move?" Her face went tight again.

A reminder for him that even if she wasn't Benji's teacher, any rogue attraction couldn't lead anywhere lasting. Which would make his proposal all the simpler. "After the holidays, once the ranch expansion project is complete, we move on to the next project."

"That sounds like so much change for a kid."

"Which brings me back to my point. I don't have time to search for another tutor. You've already made the connection with him."

Her eyes went wide with a deer-in-the-headlights look. "Mr. Fuller—"

"Call me Micah," he insisted.

"Okay, Micah."

"Good. Now hear me out. You've got an advanced degree in exactly the help that Benji needs, and I'd be only too grateful to pay you what that time is worth to us. Let me hire you to be Benji's after-school nanny and tutor." Grinning, he took a step closer, ducking his head toward hers. "You could even help with my puppy problem."

Chapter Four

I am not afraid of storms, for I am learning how to sail my ship. Susanna reached for the favorite *Little Women* quote to steady herself in the wake of Micah's question.

Because this felt like a storm.

"Be Benji's nanny?" Susanna repeated, more to give herself time to process her shock than because she wondered about misunderstanding. She'd heard loud and clear, alright. His offer had come out of left field, and she needed to figure out a way to politely decline.

Inhaling the scent of musky hay and sweet

cinnamon-infused pastries, she crossed her arms over her chest. She tuned out the noise from the band tuning up to start again, the barking of shelter dogs in the barn and children squealing with carrots in their hands eager to feed the nickering horses at the fence line.

"After school," he reminded her, his broad shoulders blocking out the festival's controlled chaos behind him. She did her best to not notice the way the sun lit his cobalt eyes. "To help you with money, help me with my crazy schedule. A mutually beneficial situation that would ultimately be the best for Benji."

For Benji? Phrasing the request that way sounded a bit like manipulation, which grated on her last nerve.

"Just so you know." She stepped closer, boots disturbing the mixture of gravel, hay and orange sprinkles from a child's cupcake, staring him down with a bravado that grew by the day. "I may be shy. I may even be timid at times. But I won't cave to being pressured by guilt."

She wasn't used to standing up for herself like this, a phenomenon that had started the day of her first showdown with this man. But she couldn't deny how empowered, how charged she felt in this moment. Sharp cold fall air prickled in her chest as she held his gaze, refusing her normal inclination to break the eye contact.

"Timid?" He smothered a laugh. "That's not a word I would ever use to describe you."

And there it was again. That crackling of tension in the air, the sense that he saw her, really saw her. Which should be a big warning bell to back away. Fast. "Thank you for the job offer and the vote of confidence in my abilities. But my answer is no."

Distress twinged the normally steady line of his lips. Such a small movement, but Susanna was always one for details.

He scrubbed the back of his neck. "What can I say to help you change your mind? Not pressure. Just persuade. I am sorry for making you feel guilted in any way. I mean that."

His words stunned her. That he would apologize—and so earnestly—was unexpected, to say the least. And in that moment, she saw how deeply he cared about his nephew. He wasn't phoning it in as Benji's guardian or trying to pawn his nephew off onto other people. He wasn't late and missing notes because he was negligent.

The guy was legitimately overwhelmed by the

big change in his life and was trying his best to search for a solution.

So where did that leave her?

Confused. Unsure what to do next. And realizing that if he was old or already married, she wouldn't hesitate to say yes to the offer to tutor Benji.

He held up a hand, his palm open to her. "You don't have to decide now. I realize this is a lot to think through. Besides, I have a puppy to pick out." He gestured to the barn teeming with people pouring in and out, the shelter's mobile vaccination van parked beside. "Any tips about what traits we should look for?"

Her anger melted, her heart softening. She couldn't help with his nanny problem, but she *could* assist in this matter. "Do you mind if I come along? It would be a lot easier to explain if I'm looking at the puppies."

His eyebrows lifted in surprise for a moment before he smiled. "I would appreciate your feedback. Thank you."

She looked past him to the expertly carved pumpkins featuring dogs running, sitting and leaping for Frisbees. She chewed her lip, the taste of clovers from warm spiced cider still lingering on her taste buds. "I do want to help Benji. I just can't be his nanny."

And as the words left her mouth, she wondered whom she was trying to convince more. Him? Or herself?

Micah hadn't won over Susanna to his nanny proposal.

Yet.

But he wasn't giving up. He took hope in her offer to pick out a puppy. He didn't intend to squander the time with her here in the barn. And lucky for him, Benji was taking his sweet time choosing.

Leaning back against a well-sanded beam, Micah crossed his arms across his chest. The space hummed with activity for the pet adoption event. The ranch sported three barns, two for animals and one for events like this one. Circular pens were stationed throughout for dogs and puppies, hay on the floor. A wall of crates showcased cats. Shelter staff guided potential adopters to different animals.

Inside one of the fenced areas, Benji sat cross-legged on the hay-strewn floor, Susanna beside him as they played with two puppies. Best he could tell, they appeared to be some kind of mountain dog mix. He could look at their info on the chalkboard, but he didn't want to take his eyes off the moment. His nephew was completely relaxed, beaming in fact. Benji's blond hair fell in front of his eyes as he stuck his hand out for one of the more active puppies to sniff.

And it was all because of the guidance of the dynamo lady looking utterly comfortable and stunning sitting on a dusty floor with a puppy in her lap and another rowdier one bouncing behind her chewing a lock of Susanna's hair.

It felt strange having help, leaning on someone else. And not just since Benji came into his life. Even before then, he'd been the responsible one growing up, although his brother, Benjamin, was older. Benjamin had struggled with drug and alcohol addiction for as long as Micah could remember. On the positive side—if one could think such a thing about having a junkie for a sibling—Micah had learned independence. Their parents had always been pulling Benjamin out of the fire, leaving Micah to learn how to take care of himself.

So it grated to ask for help from Susanna.

But that independence also produced a tenacious determination. Now that he'd decided he needed Susanna's help, he wasn't giving up until he had her firmly in his nephew's corner.

Benji picked up a neon green tug rope and fishtailed it on the floor, luring the hyper puppy. "What kind of dog did you have when you were growing up?"

In the yellow, rustic lanterns hanging in the barn, the pup crouched, tail swishing back and forth like a tiger before he launched forward—a chubby blur of black, tan and white.

Susanna scratched the fluffy mutt in her lap between the ears. The quieter puppy's deep brown eyes looked between him and Benji, until it finally let out a small yawn, the pink of the tongue a stark contrast against the white on his nose framed by tan and black.

Although both looked identical, the one who rested his head on Susanna's lap radiated a calm gentleness. "I didn't have a dog."

"A cat?" Benji tossed a toy to the energetic canine with an orange collar. Rascally little tiger sank his teeth into the little soccer ball, eliciting a small squeak from the toy.

"Nope." She shook her head, adjusting the yellow collar on the snoozing puppy. Her light-up pumpkin necklace rested on top of the dog.

"No pets at all?" His blue eyes went wide, so

focused on her that he didn't notice his shoe was being chewed.

Micah winced, already envisioning all the destruction. How could Susanna look so serene with chaos all around her?

And so very cute.

"I had a beta fish once." She eased the shoelace from the active pup's mouth.

"What's a beta fish?" Benji's face scrunched up, head tilting to the side.

"It's a bright-colored fish that lives in a clear vase with some kind of plant growing out of the water." She scooped up the hyper puppy and passed it over the fence railing to a volunteer, continuing without missing a beat. "I named him Neptune."

"After the planet?"

"Good guess," she praised, shifting the drowsy pup from her lap to his. "But Neptune is also a legendary god of water. How did you hear about the planet?"

Micah held his breath, waiting for Benji to object to losing the orange-collared maniac shoe chewer. Already, a couple had waylaid the volunteer to croon over the active fur ball.

But Benji didn't even seem to notice, he was so

intent on the librarian. He buried his fingers in the plush coat. "Uncle Micah tells me about the stars and planets when we sit outside at night. He says I seem to remember best when we talk, so he tells me. And I do remember."

Well, huh. He'd forgotten he said that.

"That's very wise of your uncle." She gazed back at him over the child's head, her gaze holding, then returning to Benji. "Which planet is your favorite?"

"Mars, because scientists think it has the biggest volcano." His voice grew more and more animated, his hand petting smoothly. "I love volcanoes and molten rock and hot lava."

"What a smart boy you are."

Beaming, Benji gathered the dog closer, looking up at Micah. "This one. Can we have this one?"

Somehow, Susanna had managed to get Benji to pick the calmest puppy in the place. Confident, not shy. And Benji even thought he'd made the choice. The lady had a gift for steering without being manipulative.

More than ever, he saw how much Benji needed her. To be truthful, *he* needed her help too. Parenting was tough. Tougher than anything he'd tackled.

He sure wouldn't mind some of that reputed Top Dog magic to persuade her.

Micah pushed off the beam, searching for something clever to say when he heard approaching boot steps through the murmur of the crowd. Turning his head, he saw the stable manager striding toward them, her braided brown hair draped over her left shoulder.

Eliza leaned into the kennel, scratching the pup's head. "Did you find a match?"

Benji looked up, smiling. "She's my new best friend forever and ever. We're going to take her home. Right, Uncle Micah?"

Micah squatted down to Benji's level, giving the calm pup a head scratch. "This is definitely the pup we want. But remember, Benji, the shelter's rules say we have to wait to pick up the puppy until Monday afternoon."

Micah appreciated the rescue's responsible approach. He'd already filled out the application and had been preapproved. He'd done so because he hadn't wanted to get Benji's hopes up, only to hit a snag. But barring the unforeseen, on Monday afternoon they would pick up their puppy.

After Benji gave the dog one last cuddle and

kiss on the head, the boy passed her over to the shelter employee.

Eliza looped her thumbs into the belt loops on her faded denim jeans. "Since you've found your puppy, I was wondering if you would like to join in on a trail ride. We've had a last-minute cancellation. I'd love it if you could come along."

Benji clapped his hands on either side of his face. "Whoa! That would be awesome."

Nodding, Eliza smiled warmly. "And I've already seen what accomplished riders you both are. We'll even be able to see the progress on the campground from a higher vantage point."

"That's right." Benji crumpled up fists of straw from the ground. "Uncle Micah loves horses. He said he was gonna teach me how to ride while we're here and now we can start."

Susanna eased to her feet, dusting hay off her leggings. "I should probably go back to check on the food donations."

Eliza waved her off. "It's totally under control. Besides, you've been here since seven this morning. You deserve a break. And don't worry about story time. It's a short ride. You'll be back well in advance."

Benji jumped up and down. "Yay!"

Micah rested a hand on the boy's shoulder. "Maybe Miss Levine has something else here she would like to enjoy. Let's don't pressure her."

Benji's face fell.

Sighing, her eyes tender, she smoothed back the boy's hair from his forehead. "I would love to go for a trail ride. It's a treat I don't get to indulge in nearly enough."

Well, how about that? It appeared the ranch had worked some of its magic for him after all with the gift of more time to make his case to Susanna. And he didn't intend to squander this chance.

By sundown, he would secure a nanny deal with Susanna Levine.

Susanna held the reins in a loose grip, tipping her face to the sunshine dappling through the branches. Pine and fir trees scented the shaded path while Whisper, a red roan gelding, clopped surefooted along the gentle dirt route through the woods.

Maybe this trail ride hadn't been the smartest of moves, extending her day with Micah and Benji Fuller. But their exchange while picking the puppy had been so effortless that she wondered if she'd been too wary, if she'd been borrowing trouble assuming the worst outcome.

So what that the boy's unattached uncle was so ruggedly good-looking it made her teeth hurt? She was a professional. Nothing had happened between them and she wouldn't allow anything to happen.

She could—and would—just enjoy this surprise opportunity for a ride. Eliza's turquoise Top Dog pullover was a beacon to follow as she guided Nutmeg, a blood bay Thoroughbred that the ranch had helped rescue and rehab from a neglect situation. Wind rippled the horse's reddish-brown mane. With Benji securely in front of him, Micah rode Goliath, a large Tennessee walking horse, calm and steady.

They'd been joined by a handful of ranch guests—New Yorkers celebrating a family reunion, commemorating the loss of their matriarch. Brown, curly hair peaked out from underneath the helmet on a woman in her midfifties. Two teenage girls with auburn curls adjusted their hands nervously on the well-worn sable leather reins. Three men who looked like echoes of each other, all clearly brothers, rode side by side.

Eliza, who was at the head of the line, pivoted in her decorated Western saddle, signaling them all to halt by raising her hand. "Thank you to everyone for joining us today. This will be a short trail ride, but we'll see the origin of the ranch's heart juxtaposed with the exciting expansion and future. In fact, the contractor has joined us today."

Micah waved sheepishly and then ruffled his nephew's hair. "My little guy here is the inspiration for the perfect family vacation. Thanks for including us, Eliza."

The easy exchange made her chest go tight, and that in itself made her even more uncomfortable. Hadn't she suggested Eliza check him out? Susanna forced a smile on her face as the stable manager continued.

"I appreciate the opportunity to share more about the magical history of our corner of the mountain. Hundreds of years ago, when the O'Brien ancestors were settling into this area, they followed a very special doe—the Queen of the Forest, glowing like starlight. Now, the O'Briens were from Scotland and Ireland so they knew the Queen of the Forest used to roam Scotland and lead wayward souls to safe places and healing water."

The two teenage girls leaned in, eyes wide and a bit starry as Eliza continued with her tale.

"Okay, so this next part is important, because those long-ago O'Briens were having a tough time settling into this region. They even wanted to give up on the land. On each other. But they followed the Queen of the Forest to a cave. I bet Benji can tell us what they found there."

"A puppy," he announced. "A lost puppy that was cold and wet and really dirty."

"That's right," Eliza confirmed, her long braid swinging in time with the horse's gait. "They cleaned up the young pup. As they rinsed the puppy together, they found their connection was back. They were healed. Perhaps our local librarian can finish up? She's read the tale to students so many times she probably knows the story better than I do."

"I'm happy to chime in," Susanna agreed. "Since then, people take the same path back to the cove that houses Sulis Springs. They leave pumpkins and fresh-cut sunflowers for the Queen of the Forest and her magic that brings people together."

One of the teenage girls half whispered, "How cool."

The woman with curly hair looked over toward

Benji, grinning. "I bet that's not all the magic in the mountain."

Benji's eyes went wide. "Do you think so?" He looked at Susanna, then back at his uncle. "Really?"

Micah nodded. "I would sure think so."

Benji asked, "Are all legends true? Miss Levine?"

"Not all are true. Some are outright made-up stories. And some have bits of truth woven into the tale." As she explained, an idea took root. She looked toward Eliza, thinking of how much Benji retained from his talk with Micah under the stars. "How about we create a legend now? Provided the others don't mind. Eliza?"

"What a great idea. I would love to hear it." She waved for the party to continue on the path that was growing thick with red, yellow and orange maple and oak leaves. The others on horseback nodded in agreement, drawing closer on the trail ride. Micah was so near, the breeze carried the tempting scent of his aftershave.

Benji chewed his bottom lip, his forehead furrowed. "Like, how would we make a legend?"

Now, this was her wheelhouse. "I'll start. Imagine that there are fairies and gnomes out there."

"In the trees?" Benji pointed, shifting in the saddle. "Under that log there?"

Micah steadied his nephew, with a broad but gentle hand. "Careful there, buddy."

Susanna had to drag her gaze off the tender tableau before she got whacked with a branch and fell off her own horse. "Once upon a time, before even the legend of Moonlight Ridge came to be, there was a little gnome named—"

"Named Benji. Like me," he squealed enthusiastically, gripping the saddle horn.

"A little gnome named Benji. He loved horses and dogs and playing in the forest. And he was such a very smart boy, he knew the names of all the plants and animals." Susanna paused, shooting an encouraging glance at Micah.

Nodding, Micah joined in. "Benji the gnome made a house in a hollowed-out spot on an oak tree. Because Benji was so small, there was a lot of room in his tree home, so he invited a chipmunk named…"

"Patrice!" Benji shouted.

"Yes," Micah continued. "Benji the gnome invited Patrice the chipmunk, who had been wandering in the forest all alone, to live with him. They started to become a family and took many great adventures together."

Susanna nodded, impressed and surprised at Micah's quick creativity. She couldn't miss the way Micah was forming a family with Benji, bringing the boy into his life and adapting to fatherhood. "One time, Benji and Patrice walked on a log to cross over a babbling brook. Benji learned the sweetest blueberries of forest were over that log and he knew that was Patrice's favorite sweet treat... Micah, what do you think happened next?"

"Well, once they crossed the log, Patrice stuffed three blueberries in her mouth so she looked like this." Micah puffed out his cheeks as Benji peered up at him from the saddle.

Laughter bubbled inside her, his deep chuckles swelling around her. And while she registered on some level that others were laughing too, her focus was locked on him. On his broad shoulders. The stubble along his jaw.

The blue-flame heat of his cobalt eyes.

A gasp teased the edge of her mind, followed by a squeal from Benji.

"Uncle Micah, look." The boy pointed toward the valley, at the campground construction in progress.

A family of bears were flipping trash cans, climbing on the backhoe and toppling a pile of lumber.

Chapter Five

With his life's savings riding on making this job a success, Micah wasn't waiting around for someone else to mosey on down to disperse the three bears trashing his construction site.

He clutched the reins, the horse's hooves pounding earth on the way to the campground in progress. Ducking his head to dodge a low-hanging branch, he tried not to think too hard about the mounting damage from that small family of black bears and how much time and money it would cost to repair. The stable manager was calling the park ranger and Jacob O'Brien. With luck, one of them would arrive before him.

Susanna was keeping watch over Benji. Thank God she'd been on hand for him to pass over the boy. He trusted her and knew Benji wouldn't panic in her care. No doubt, his nephew still carried some abandonment issues from all he'd been through.

The kid needed—deserved—the best. And to make that happen, Micah had to keep his business afloat. This was his big breakout project, which meant his finances were already stretched. If Micah had to toss those marauding animals off the property single-handedly, he would do it.

A snap of fall wind darted through the cuffs of his flannel. Maybe it was just nerves over the bears threatening his and Benji's future, or maybe it was the bitter chill on the breeze, but his hairs stood on end. So different from the mild fall days of midseventies in the South. Then again, he didn't have to worry about a furry trio disrupting work sites there either. Just snakes.

Following the paw print signs on the pine trees, he rounded the last bend into the construction zone by a creek. Mama bear was in fine form flinging a trash can. Of course, it landed square on a pallet of windows earmarked for the rec cabin. A brown fuzzy cub crawled around under the trailer that served as temporary office space. He would have laughed at the other cub on the backhoe seat except the little fella was batting at the gears on a seventy-five-thousand-dollar piece of equipment.

Dismounting, he made fast work of tying his horse's reins to a tree, a safe distance away. He scooped up a wrench and the lid to a trash can. It wasn't the same as a bear whistle or horn, but it would have to do until someone else arrived.

He clanged the wrench against the metal lid, drumming loud and fast, waving his arms to make himself look larger.

"Scram, go, get away," he shouted at the bears, voice carrying and echoing.

Mama uncurled to her full height and stared him in the eyes for four heavy heartbeats. The beast's breath puffed into the chilly air. There was no backing down now. Micah hammered the lid a final time. Mama slouched again, pivoted away and lumbered back toward the tree line, her two cubs falling in file behind her.

Exhaling, Micah dropped his makeshift gong on the ground just as Jacob O'Brien jogged out of the forest, bear horn in one hand and bear spray in the other. Micah gave himself a moment of relief before assessing the damage.

"Hey, Fuller," Jacob called out. "Are you okay? Hollie called me about the bear sighting."

"All clear." Huffing from his horse drew his attention and he strode back over to settle Goliath, smoothing a hand along the velvety neck. "Mama and her two cubs headed back into the woods."

"That's a relief. I'll just let Hollie and the others know." He texted fast, then tucked his cell in his pocket. "Any damage?"

"Tough to tell for sure until I clean up the mess. I'll take care of that today though."

Jacob set the bear deterrents on a picnic table. "Will this delay the grand opening in December?"

"I'll have crews working round the clock if need be." Which meant overtime pay and more hours away from Benji.

More than ever, he needed to persuade Susanna to help out with Benji. The ranch's day care was great for playmates and activities, but it wasn't going to get the job done with his tutoring.

"Sorry this happened. But bears are a fact of life around here." Jacob bent over to clear various bits of debris. Wood planks were scattered about, the slightly muddy dirt making the scene look even more chaotic. "It looks to me like you're very careful about trash disposal. I see locking lids on your company's cans, with bags inside."

Micah picked up a piece of metal, the cold against his skin intensified by the bite in the air. "All are empty and from what I've observed you haul away trash every day."

"It could just be an unfortunate accident," Jacob conceded, pausing as he followed a trail of... French fries? Leading to a cut section of orange plastic construction fencing. "Or..."

"Something deliberate?" But why?

Jacob scrubbed a hand along his jaw. "It just seems odd. We're careful with garbage pickup and the place was cordoned off." He dangled the severed fencing from his hand. "This just looks so purposeful. Almost like Hansel and Gretel breadcrumbs. Do you have anyone with a grudge against you or your company?"

A grudge against the company? He wouldn't say that exactly. Last he'd heard, Benji's mom Lola was still in treatment. And sure, his brother hated him because of Benji's custody case and restricted, supervised visitation—even though the boy had been moved to the grandparents first. But his brother wasn't the sort to trash a site. Benjamin was more likely to call in the middle of the night to chew him out.

But expend effort by actually showing up to hash out a problem? Nah. "Doubtful that anyone would have done this to me on purpose." If anything, his brother seemed to turn up like a bad penny at happy occasions with Lola at his side, both of them stoned. "But I'll review the surveillance camera footage from the site. Maybe add security to the equipment and office trailer."

All costly for a project that was already stretching him to the limit. But he couldn't afford for this eco-friendly campground to be anything other than a huge success.

The weight of responsibility sucker punched him all over again. Rubbing a hand along the tight knot gathering in his chest, he looked around at the mess and realized how reckless he'd been confronting the bears on his own. If something happened to him, Benji would have no one.

A hand on his shoulder startled him back into the present, shifting his attention to Jacob again and restoring order to his world. He'd had enough with being jerked around by life today.

"Well, Fuller, maybe the animals just want you to stick around. But on to a more pressing question…"

Jacob fixed him with a knowing stare. "What's the deal with you and Susanna Levine?"

Benji's stomach hurt. Bad. Why didn't anyone know what had happened with Uncle Micah yet? It had been a long time since they cut the ride short and sent him back to the ranch, adding him to an activity with Top Dog guests and the Hudson kids.

Like making dog cookies would distract him?

Well, it did. Sort of. Because he was going to save some for his new puppy.

Guitar music drifted through the yellow-and-orange tent. Benji bobbed his head up and down—there was finally a song that he liked playing. Miss Levine was helping measure out the ingredients into different containers for the kids to mix. But she looked worried as she was talking to Mrs. O'Brien and some of the other moms.

And that made his tummy hurt more.

At the long, wooden table, he carefully mixed pumpkin and mashed bananas into his spiderweb-themed mixing bowl. Lips pressed tight, Benji did his best to stay focused. Though the baaaa-ing of the white goat in the petting zoo kept breaking his concentration. The mixture was getting really sticky on his wooden spoon.

Mrs. O'Brien had told them they could also use peanut butter if they made it at home, but that wasn't okay here today because some kid might have a peanut allergy. He didn't want to make anybody sick but peanut butter was his favorite and he was bummed he couldn't include it for his puppy.

Benji leaned forward, his forearms pressing into the wood while Ivy and her twin brothers investigated their own concoction next to him. Ivy pushed her light pink glasses up the bridge of her nose.

Phillip adjusted his blue baseball cap as his face scrunched. "Are they sure it's bears? I thought bears started hibernating around here this time of year."

Elliot tapped his fingers on the table, shaking his head. His red shirt with a pug on it was really loose and a couple of times he'd pulled his arms all the way inside and flapped the sleeves. "Not all of them."

"Well," Phillip said, "mama bears don't have babies this time of year."

Elliot sighed. "It takes them a while to be full grown up."

Ivy shuffled over to Benji's bowl, peering inside to investigate how many lumps were left in the batter. "I bet somebody left their food out."

Benji's stomach flipped again, and his eyes stung. He tucked his face fast and scrubbed his sleeve across. The last thing he needed was people calling him crybaby *and* dummy. "Maybe it was me who left the food out. I didn't eat all my sandwich today."

Phillip dropped the wooden spoon. "It wasn't your lunch box. You left it at school."

Oh, yeah. He forgot. He'd gotten to the bus to come to the ranch's after-school program and realized he'd left his new lunchbox in the classroom. But he was a bus rider, and they loaded up first. The car riders who got picked up by their parents stayed in the room waiting to go second.

Curtis was a car rider.

Benji hadn't wanted to go back in there and risk getting made fun of again.

Ivy wiped some dough on her waist apron that was decorated with dancing poodles and pumpkins. "Well, even if you had left some food, I know you wouldn't have done it on purpose."

"You don't gotta make excuses for me. I'm not a baby."

Ivy's face fell and she smooshed a cookie cutter hard into the dough. "You don't have to be mean."

Her sad face made him feel bad. She really deserved to have a real friend. One who could read smart books like she did so they could talk about what happened.

"I'm sorry." Benji shifted on his feet, squeezing his hands around the smooth spatula. He might as well let her off the hook. "I know you're only being nice to me because your mom made you."

"That's not true. You're my friend. I'll prove it too. Friends tell each other secrets." She leaned in and said softly, "She's not really my mom."

Benji's eyes went wide and his heart pounded. "What do you mean?"

"My parents died." She chewed her bottom lip for a second before starting again. "The O'Briens are adopting me and my brothers. Our last name isn't even really O'Brien yet. But the school lets us use it so we don't feel different."

It had never occurred to him before now that he was lucky Uncle Micah had his same last name. They were family, and that was a good thing. "Well, my parents aren't dead."

Phillip tipped his head. "Then why do you live with your uncle?"

Ivy lowered her voice, glaring at her brother. Then she gave a small smile to Benji that said she was on his side. "That's not our business."

Thinking about his mom and dad made him feel weird inside. Like he should stick up for them. But he knew Ivy didn't mean to make him feel bad.

Maybe she'd understand better than most people.

"I have lots of family. Sometimes I live with my mom and dad." He didn't remember much about his parents. His mom pushing him on a swing. His dad throwing snowballs. Then there was the day the police came to their apartment and he got taken away. "And sometimes I live with my grand-parents."

Ivy lifted the ghost cookie cutter up, grinning slightly at the clean lines in the dough. "And now you're with your uncle?"

"Right." And he was glad. It was better with his uncle. But it was also embarrassing. Like being called dummy.

"When do you go back to your mom and dad?"

His tummy went tight, really tight. And just as they announced story time, he shot to his feet...

And threw up all over his dog cookies.

* * *

Susanna gathered up her collection of Biscuit the Dog children's books while Atlas snoozed on the fluffy bed at her feet. His little paws twitched slightly, and she imagined that Atlas was dreaming of a big open field. Her story time booth had been set up to a covered wagon with treats for the kids, near the barn and petting zoo, reminding her of all the ways stories seemed to come more alive in the outdoors.

Benji had sure recovered quickly from his upset stomach during cookie making. He confessed to having eaten seven of the people cookies—not dog cookies, he insisted. Since he didn't have a fever and kept down a snack of mini corn dogs, she'd called Micah and they'd agreed to let him rejoin the play.

Working in tandem to take care of him had felt too easy today. So much so, she'd made a point of handing him over into Hollie's care once story time ended.

With luck, she could slip out before Micah found her to finish the conversation about being Benji's tutor. She needed space from the too-cute contractor and his heart-tugging nephew. Her gaze skated to the pumpkin patch, where the kids were having a dance party to work their wriggles out after story time. Seeing him at ease with others now drew such a contrast to how much he struggled at school fit in.

Could that have factored into his upset stomach?

A river of families walked between her booth and the kids, carrying the sweet scent of candied apples, cinnamon spice cider and relational connection. A little girl with black braids paused in front of her table, corn dog in one hand and a stuffed animal that looked a lot like Atlas in another. She squealed, pointed and whispered to her mom. Susanna smiled, waving at them both as they walked by heading out of the adoption event.

Elsewhere, the grounds were filled with the shelter staff breaking down pens, crating animals. A roar of chatter mixed in with the country music piping through the sound system.

This day had been so very different from what she'd expected when she rolled out of bed to help with the food drive and lead a couple of story hours. No matter how much she tried to delude herself into thinking she should keep her distance from Micah Fuller, the universe kept tossing them together.

Why couldn't he be a jerk? That would have made him a lot easier to resist.

Like now.

His long-legged stride ate up the space between them and the laser focus in his blue eyes on her made it clear he knew exactly where he was going. So much for slipping out before another conversation.

With only a passing wave at the ranch staff who called out to him, he reached to rest a hand on her arm to stop her. "Do you have a minute?"

Her skin tingled at the contact, even through her sweater. "I, uh, really need to get Atlas home soon."

"I'll make it quick. Scout's honor." He grinned, his hand sliding away. "Thanks for making sure Benji was settled while I took care of the three bears. How's he feeling?"

"He seems right as rain. I'm glad I was there to help. I'm just sorry it happened." She toyed with the strap on her book sack. "How bad is the damage?"

"It's not good. Could have been worse. I'll figure it out." His face creased with stress, and he stuffed his hands in his jacket pocket, his gaze sliding to his nephew and back. "I was impressed with the way you got Benji to build a story during our ride."

She'd known Benji was smart right from the start and that impression only grew stronger. He was a gifted storyteller. "He's a smart boy who's hungry to learn."

"I'm glad to hear you say that." He sighed. Hard. His relief evident. "It's time to pick up where we left off in our earlier conversation."

"What do you mean?" She backed away, securing her hold on the dog leash and book bag.

"About my offer for you to be his caretaker and tutor after school. I'll pay you well for your time."

She cleared her throat, trying not to notice the way the breeze ruffled his wavy hair. "So we're really discussing this."

"I'm dead serious. I need your help and I overheard you talking about being short of cash. This solves problems for both of us."

As much as she needed the money, she couldn't afford the risk to her calm and secure new start. She had to make her "no" politely clear. "I appreciate the offer and your care for your nephew. But I can't quit my job."

"That's why I said 'after school.' Whatever that

would look like—he stays with you after the bell or you pick him up and work with him until I'm off."

"Micah—"

"Just wait. Let me finish. You'll call the shots. However many days a week after school. And while I don't mind helping Benji with his homework, I wish we had more time for R & R." His love and concern for Benji shone through every word. "Having you help with his reading and homework would give me that flexibility."

"Micah," she said, crossing her arms across her chest like a shield against his charm. "I can't."

He continued as if she hadn't spoken. "We've already discussed why you're the best for the job given our upcoming move. Don't say no."

And just as he reminded her of the reasons she needed to keep her distance, he also managed to pull at her heartstrings for his nephew. She knew too well how hard it was to fit in each time. And kids already teased Benji for his reading difficulties. What would happen at the next place where he didn't have the built-in support of the O'Brien kids?

Saying no was getting harder and harder. "I'll think about it."

"You're still on the fence?" he asked, incredulous. "Even though you've said you need the money? Do you have a problem with me?"

Oh, she had plenty of problems with him and the attraction to his lumberjack body and how he crept up on her defenses with the way he tried so hard with his nephew.

She opted to ignore his question. More because she needed to get away from his allure. "I'll let you know my decision by tomorrow morning."

Hitching her bag on her shoulder, she pivoted away only to find Benji looking back and forth between them.

"What decision?" he asked.

She looked at his freckled face, smudged with chocolate, his wary eyes the same color blue as his uncle's. Her mind echoed with memories of all the times he struggled to read while the other children snickered. And how because of that, he had difficulty making friends. Her heart broke for Benji—not for the first time—and she just couldn't let him feel one more rejection.

Not when it was in her power to help make his life easier.

She sighed in surrender. "Starting Monday, I'm going to be your after-school nanny."

But no way, no how would she be anything more to the boy's uncle.

Chapter Six

"Aren't they such a precious family?" a voice carried on the breeze.

The words drifted over to Micah, freezing him as he lifted the puppy carrier from his truck, his gaze meeting—holding—Susanna's on top of the plastic crate. He scanned to the cabin porch and found that the words came from an older couple on their porch, dressed in matching red plaid sweaters. Micah stifled a wince and didn't bother correcting the woman pointing in their direction. She and her husband were simply Top Dog guests, so the observation didn't really matter.

Other than the fact the words made Susanna look like she'd just had a near miss from a bear. Her face went pale, her Cupid's bow lips pressing together.

Clearing her throat, she eased away a step and turned fast to help unbuckle Benji from his booster chair in the back seat of Micah's extended-cab truck. "Come on, kiddo. Let's get you down so we can welcome your puppy home."

Their new furry friend yipped in agreement from inside the carrier.

Benji jumped up and down with excitement. "Can I play with her? Please, please?"

Micah thumbed the truck's key fob to lock the vehicle. "Once we get in the yard."

The deep blue autumn sky contrasted with the pine frame of the cabin—complete with a picket fence he'd constructed to make his time here with Benji easier. A tire swing hung from the far-reaching branch of an oak tree with a toy dump truck underneath.

Micah had made an effort here, trying his best to provide a home for the boy who deserved one. He wondered if Susanna recognized any of that, or if she still viewed him as the dad who wasn't doing enough to help his boy.

It rattled him to realize how much her good opinion meant.

"What are you going to name your puppy?"

Benji practically exploded with excitement as he clapped his hands together. "I get to choose?"

The way his nephew responded to what felt like a standard rite of passage for kids pained him. Benji's last few years had been rough and Micah didn't doubt that Benji sensed that he didn't have any control of his life for so long.

Going forward, Micah resolved to look for more opportunities for him to have some autonomy. "Of course you do."

He just hoped it wasn't something awful. With breath held, he waited.

Benji knelt in front of the crate and poked a finger through the grate, stroking a furry paw. The puppy yawned, her pink tongue curling. "Hmm. I think I want to name her Jupiter. Because I love planets."

Susanna clapped, looking mouthwateringly cute in her poncho sweater with a bat clip. "That's an awesome choice. I love it."

Micah tore his gaze away and adjusted his hold on the pet carrier. Man, the puppy was heavy. Twenty pounds, according to the adoption paperwork, which included a vet visit and vaccination records. "Let's get Jupiter into the fenced area so she can run around for a while and you can play with her."

Susanna unlatched the gate, swinging it wide for Benji. "Did you know that Jupiter is also a name from mythology?"

Micah followed, his gaze gravitating right back to the hypnotic sway of her hips in jeans, her braid swishing as she walked. Setting the crate on the ground, he kept his silence to listen while Susanna worked her magic with Benji.

The little boy's eyes went wide. "Really? Like Zeus?"

"Zeus is a Greek god," Susanna explained patiently, in a manner that didn't deflate confidence. "Jupiter is a god from Roman mythology. He's the god of thunder and sky."

"If Jupiter is a god and not a goddess, does that mean it's a boy name? My puppy is a girl."

Susanna glanced at Micah.

"Fine by me," he said.

Nodding, she turned back to Benji. "It's completely okay to name your dog Jupiter. Can you think of names that are for both boys and girls?"

"Yeah, I have kids like that in my class." He

counted on his fingers. "Dakota and Jamie and Shawn and Drew and Taylor."

"That's exactly right."

"Cool," he said before shifting his focus fast to his new best friend. "Come on, Jupiter, follow me. There's a ball over here."

Leaves crunched under Benji's black cowboy boots as he ran through the yard. Simple joy carved a smile onto his nephew's face as Jupiter bounded behind him, her tail wagging. Childish laughter clung in the brisk air as Jupiter circled a basketball. Tail wagging, Jupiter assessed the ball before launching forward. The pup landed on the top of the ball, perfectly balanced.

Since Benji was happy and occupied, Micah decided to make the most of the free moment.

"Sit for a minute?" He gestured for Susanna to have a seat on one of two Adirondack chairs on either side of a firepit.

She hesitated for a moment before nodding and choosing the chair closest to the tire swing. "Sure. I left Atlas with Eliza while we were getting the dog. She said he's welcome to stay as long as I need. I'll just send her a text."

"Thank you for coming along to the shelter this afternoon." He lowered himself into the other chair, trying not to think overlong on how nice it was to share the moment with her, to see the sunset shining through her hair.

"Well, I am your new nanny." As she tapped out a quick text, she stretched her legs, her Halloween socks peeking from the top of her leather ankle boots.

"I realize that puppy pickup isn't listed in your new job description." He rested a booted foot on the stacked rocks around the firepit.

"Building a relationship with Benji is important. I'll work this into a lesson. And it will all be fun." She traced a slim finger along the arm of her chair. "Besides, my afternoon was free. You're the one who had to take off work early."

"It was worth it." He gestured to his nephew leaning against the fences, the pup prancing through the yellow-orange leaves.

He couldn't help but notice the way Susanna's eyes tracked Benji and Jupiter, a small smile tugging at the corner of her mouth. A smile Benji returned in a flash.

Susanna leaned forward on her knees, braid falling from behind her back to touch her arm in a tempting sweep. "Getting your first pet is such a milestone. Thank you for including me in this special moment in Benji's life."

"Didn't you say Atlas is your first dog?" Micah opened his wallet, pulling out a key. The firepit supplies were safely locked away in the end table between his seat and Susanna's.

"I promised myself that once I got settled, I would get a pet of my own. When I first started working here, I had Hollie's dog in my class. And I was hooked." She shrugged, picking up a twig off the ground and tossing it into the firepit. "Now I have Atlas with me every day at work, which is amazing. Did you have pets growing up?"

Fitting the bronze key into the lock, he jiggled it until the latch caught and the metal door squeaked open. Building a fire would give him something to focus on besides Susanna's growing appeal.

"We had horses." Grateful for an excuse to avoid her too-perceptive eyes, Micah concentrated on pulling the lighter from the shallow cabinet, his fingers pressing into the steel handle of the lighter. As a kid, he'd wanted a dog. But his mother wouldn't allow one in the house because of the fur and he hadn't felt right about making a dog stay outside all the time.

"But what about a dog or a cat…or a hamster?"

"We had exotic fish." Fish that lived in a massive decorative tank, all color coordinated to match his mother's decor. "I named them John, Paul, George and Ringo."

"That's cute and so creative too."

Such a simple compliment, but it made him smile on the inside. He leaned forward in his seat, clicking the lighter until the starter log caught fire. He carefully fed the flame. Yellowish-orange flames covered the chunk of wood, roaring to life. "I'm glad to have the chance to teach Benji how to ride while we're at the Top Dog Dude Ranch. Like my grandmother taught me."

"Tell me more about her." She angled forward to hold her hands near the baby blaze, the temperature dropping as the sun dipped farther behind the trees.

"She was eccentric." Micah scrubbed the back of his neck, all too aware of her gaze lingering on his arms as he tossed another log onto the fire. "You never would have guessed she had money to burn. And I mean that as a compliment. She taught me to be proud of the things I built with my own two hands."

"Like what?" She tugged her braid over her shoulder and toyed with the end.

Good memories wheeled through his brain. "One summer, we constructed a chicken coop together."

That was the kind of thing he could share with Benji one day. He had no doubt his nephew would love that kind of project.

"Seriously?" Her chocolate brown eyes lit with amusement.

"Yes, ma'am," he said, sinking into both the chair and into the memory. "In my mom's backyard. I half suspect my grandmother encouraged me just to get a dig in on my mom. My parents wanted me to be an accountant."

Her eyebrows pinched together. "I have trouble picturing that."

"Funny thing, though, I have an accounting degree to go with my engineering degree."

And, now that he thought about it, Benji would have had as much trouble earning his parents' approval as Micah had. Yet another reason he was glad to step into the parent void left when his parents couldn't handle guardianship of their grandson.

Susanna's eyes widened as she nodded in approval. "Well, color me impressed. Good for you. You're quite the Renaissance man."

Her praise warmed him. It shouldn't matter what she thought of him. But it did.

The fire crackling between them echoed the snap in his blood. His every breath filled with the sultry mix of smoke and her spicy apple-sweet scent. And there was no denying...

He wanted a taste.

Her pupils went wide with an answering awareness. One that he knew if he acted upon, he would lose the best thing to happen to his nephew in a very long time. Benji's well-being had to come first.

He shoved to his feet. "What do you say we help wear out Jupiter?"

A week into her nanny-ing gig, Susanna wondered why she had worried so much about taking this job. Micah hadn't come close to making a move on her. In fact, she'd decided she must have imagined that simmering moment when their gazes had met over the firepit.

That should have made it easier to focus on her work with Benji.

But it didn't.

Holding Atlas's leash, she leaned against a tree, waiting while Benji searched for nature's debris to make a bird's nest. Puppy Jupiter was sleeping at the cabin.

Benji was a sponge when it came to learning, like he'd been starved up to now because of his struggles. Not that she faulted the teacher. He was still young to be identified with a learning disability.

And it hadn't been easy coming up with ways to make his homework less of a confidence shredder.

She'd added letters to the home in every form possible—from magnet letters on the refrigerator to ABC SpaghettiOs. They'd traced letters on Bubble Wrap. They'd studied spelling words by drawing them in shaving cream, sand and even in the dirt with a stick and sung them while dancing. For other homework, they'd used multicolor sidewalk chalk to write on stepping-stones.

By day three, she'd noticed a shift in him. His eyes didn't sheen with unshed tears as often. By the end of the week, he'd actually asked to start homework. So she'd opted for the outdoor-nest-building STEM activity as a reward.

Benji crouched, bag in one hand. "I found a feather." Standing, he held the brown quill on one hand. "Can I put that in my nest?"

"Hmm. Let's check the list…" She knelt beside

him, cupping her phone in one hand, pointing to each word as she read out loud. "Twigs, moss and, yes, here it says feathers."

"Even if the feather isn't from the baby bird's mom?" he asked. "Would it still feel at home?"

She heard layers in the question that went deeper than just a school project. But then so often, that was the case. The real problem came in assuming those complexities weren't present in speaking with kids.

"Absolutely," she said, rising, waiting for him to stand, too, before resuming their walk toward the lodge. She hoped he would keep talking if they were moving and he didn't feel pressured. "Homes can look different. That's what makes each one special."

"Like how I lived with my mom and dad. Then with my grandparents." He swung his bag back and forth, higher and faster with each word. Atlas trotted along on the leash, chasing shadows. "And now I'm with my uncle since he's sorta my new dad?"

She swallowed down the lump in her throat, but it didn't come close to easing the constriction in her chest. "That's a good example."

"How about we build some birdhouses too?

Uncle Micah can show us how. He's a good builder."

Benji looked at her with such hope in his eyes she knew there was only one answer. "Of course."

"Yay," he cheered. Benji jumped up and down, the bag flapping just as they stepped out of the woods, the Top Dog main lodge coming into view.

A sprawling garden wrapped around the side, shielding what Susanna knew was the owners' private entrance. An arbor covered in vines gave a slight peek in to Hollie and her daughter sitting at a wrought iron table.

"Ivy! Ivy!" Benji shouted, breaking free. "Check out what I found."

Benji bolted headlong toward the collection of orange and white pumpkins tucked in the small, secluded garden. Ivy sprung up from the table, racing toward her friend. Susanna trailed after, Atlas close at her heels. A flurry of leaves moving like a boat wake behind them all. Hollie pulled her plaid poncho tighter as she rose, giving Benji a quick hug before the kids sat cross-legged on the tiled patio sifting through his bag of nesting treasures.

Susanna sucked in a deep breath, the cold air stinging her lungs. "I'm sorry we disrupted you."

Hollie waved away the concern. "No need to

apologize. We were finished anyway. I've been wanting to catch up with you but you've been so busy and I've been so busy." She gestured to the table. "How did it go this week?"

How did it go? Her senses came alive with memories of accidental brushes as she and Micah had angled sideways through the little cabin kitchen. Or when he palmed her back as she walked ahead of him onto the porch. The thoughtful way he opened her car door for her. Old-fashioned maybe. But touching.

And all recollections that would give Hollie fodder for speculation. Susanna wanted no part of that.

So she focused on Benji instead. "The first day, we picked up the puppy and played, just getting to know the routine. The rest of the week has gone well."

"I'm sure that's because you're making the lessons fun. Ivy says all subjects are more interesting when you lead the discussion." Hollie spun a pencil on the table, smiling. "So, when you say 'we' got the pup, do you mean Micah too? I seem to recall he took time off Monday afternoon."

"Yes," she said, quickly shifting the subject by pointing toward the two children. "Today, we were gathering things from nature that a bird would use to build a nest, then checking them off the list."

Hollie spun the pencil faster for a moment, as if considering pushing the point, then nudged it aside. "I'm glad you can be there for Benji."

"Your resort is perfect for a child who's a tactile and auditory learner." She would have loved an experience like this as a child. But there hadn't been the money. And then when she was old enough to ride the bus and volunteer somewhere similar, her mom had gotten sick and Susanna had needed to care for her. She wasn't complaining. Her parents had sacrificed so much for her. She'd never had to question if she was loved.

Like Benji did.

Hollie toyed with the zipper tab on her Top Dog jacket. "We do try to appeal to the senses here at the Top Dog Dude Ranch."

"Like with grounding?" Susanna asked.

"Absolutely. We tend to think of it in those times someone intentionally dials into grounding to deal with anxiety or tension. But we can also use it in our day-to-day life to preemptively peel away those negative emotions before they get out of control."

"Now that I think of it," Susanna said, an idea forming, "that could be helpful with students like Benji who find schoolwork stressful."

"That's a great point. You're welcome to join in any activities here, if you wish. On your own or with Benji."

"I appreciate that. But Micah has hired me to be Benji's tutor, not playmate." Even as the excuse rolled off her tongue, Susanna couldn't avoid the knowing gleam in Hollie's eyes that said she wasn't buying the brush-off for a moment.

"Well, the offer stands if you decide the opportunity is there to weave it into his studies." Hollie reached across the table into her portfolio notebook and pulled out a brochure. "Here's a list of our October and November offerings. There are plenty of events for couples too."

As Susanna took the pamphlet, Hollie's knowing smile made Susanna realize what a poor job she was doing at hiding her fascination with Micah. A draw that wasn't going away as the spent more time together.

All the more reason to double down in her efforts to keep the relationship with Micah completely professional and nothing more.

* * *

Micah threw his truck into Park outside his cabin, cursing the latest string of animal-caused mishaps that had set his project behind. Today's batch of accidents? A skunk had sprayed three of his best workers. A hawk pooped on his blueprints. And a raccoon chewed through the wiring on his favorite circular saw—thank goodness it wasn't plugged in.

As if he wasn't already frustrated beyond measure by how distant Susanna had been.

Over the past two weeks, Susanna had grown quieter and quieter. He knew he could be gruff at times, especially when he was stressed, like now, and he hated the thought that he'd put her on edge.

Snagging his lunchbox off the seat next to him and throwing open the door, he stepped out of the truck. His boots hammering the ground with a weary thud echoed by the rolling thunder in the distance. The cabin lights shone through the dark, the moon muted by clouds.

Each porch step creaked beneath him as he hurried to close the space between him and the door before the deluge. He was no sooner turning the door handle and hurrying inside before an ominous thunder roll sounded, bringing a curtain of rain plummeting to the ground.

Inside, he found Susanna on the floor, legs tucked to the side. Atlas was curled against his couch while Jupiter rested her head on Susanna's lap as she read. Benji was so engrossed it was easy to forget how much the kid hated reading.

Micah allowed himself a moment to just soak in the peaceful scene, the perfect end to a rotten day. His eyes lingered on her slim fingers toying with the end of her braid secured by a bow adorned with books and dogs. Her subtle curves were hugged by orange, checkered slim-cut pants and a long-sleeved tee with the word *BOO* scrolled across in gold glitter. As she read, she wriggled her toes inside the socks.

He cleared back a lump in his throat and stifled the surge of desire.

Susanna startled, her hands gripping the book. "Oh, hello."

Benji pushed off the ground like a rocket, his footsteps loud on the pine floor as he ran, flinging his arms open for a hug. Jupiter and Atlas were close on his heels. "Uncle Micah, Uncle Micah. Where were you?"

"Sorry I ran late, buddy." He gathered Benji into

a bear hug, then shifted his attention to Susanna. "We were trying to get as much done as possible before the storm rolled in. We didn't expect it to hold off this long."

"You don't need to apologize." Susanna crouched, sliding off the superheroes blanket she and Benji had been sitting on. She swept it into her arms as she stood, holding it close to her chest while rose crept into her cheeks. "I'll just get out of your way and head home."

This was as good a time as any to try to smooth over whatever had made her upset with him. He didn't want Benji picking up on the tension.

And, to be truthful, he didn't like getting the cold shoulder. "The rain's coming down pretty hard. Do you want to hang out and have supper until it eases up?"

She chewed her bottom lip. "I don't want to impose."

"Please, please, Miss Levine. We're having spaghetti and meatballs." Benji tugged her hand.

Maybe this was a lost cause. "Perhaps Miss Levine has other plans."

Atlas darted under the sofa with the puppy as if he didn't want to leave. And for once, Micah didn't mind if the animals were conspiring.

"Actually," Susanna said, still hugging the wadded-up blanket in her arms, "if you're sure you don't mind, I would like to stay. You're right about the rain. The mountain roads can be treacherous in this kind of downpour."

"Great," he said, the tension rolling off his shoulders for the first time in nearly two weeks. "I'll put the finishing touches on supper."

"What can I do to help?"

He almost told her to just put her feet up, but she had a look that said she would argue, so he asked, "Set the table?"

"Sure—"

The rest of her words were swallowed by a squeak of surprise as the power went out. Plunging them into total darkness. His frustration cranked into overdrive again.

"Everyone just stay where you are and I'll find a flashlight." He extended his arms, reaching to pat and search…

Only to find his palms filled with the unmistakable softness of perfect B-cup breasts.

Chapter Seven

It had been a long time since she'd felt a man's hands on her body, even if it was accidental on his part. With the power outage and the storm pounding, her senses narrowed to just the feel of Micah's touch, savoring in the moment where there was no chance of anyone seeing. The tingle seared all the way to the roots of her hair, like she'd had a near miss with lightning.

What a shame this was completely the wrong man and the wrong time.

Clearing her throat, Susanna backed up. Only to have her feet tangle up in the puppy. Jupiter let out a yip just as she fell forward, right into Micah's arms.

"Careful there," he said, his voice a notch lower, his warm breath caressing her neck.

Heating her insides.

Strong arms tightening briefly before he released her again. But she let her palms linger on his chest for a moment, savoring the texture of his flannel shirt warmed by his body.

"Uh, thanks for keeping me from falling on my face." She eased away, more carefully this time. Her heart pounded in her ears as loudly as the rain hammered the roof. Susanna reached for the sofa, patting until she found it, lowering herself.

"Benji?" Micah called, turning on his cell phone flashlight. The thin beam swept through the dark. "Where are you, buddy?"

"I'm sitting on the kitchen floor with Atlas. I'm not moving until I can really see where I'm going," he said, a shadowy form rocking slowly with his arms around Atlas and Jupiter. "I don't wanna step on the dogs."

"Smart fella," she said dryly, still stinging from the embarrassment of having Micah's hands on her breasts.

"Okay." Micah's whiskey-rich voice blanketed

the dimly lit air. Only a hint of moonlight streamed through the window, a low flicker of flames in the fireplace. "You two stay right where you are while I look for flashlights for everyone."

Susanna hugged a throw pillow to her chest, her skin still tingling from his touch, wanting a repeat more than she wanted her own supersized flashlight. "Are you sure you don't need my help?"

"I'm good," he answered, the sound of his boots thudding along the hardwood floors. "It's easier if we aren't all tripping over each other."

Wasn't that the truth.

"Okay," Benji said. "I'm gonna stomp my feet over and over so you can hear me and you don't step on me. I don't wanna get squished."

"Good idea," Micah said, his thin stream of light bobbing forward.

A few more steps later, she heard a drawer open, then the rattle of things being shifted around. Finally, a wider shaft of light cut through the pitch-dark of the cabin. The glow swept around, lowering as Micah knelt by Benji, passing him the two flashlights. "Could you take one to Susanna, please?"

"Sure," he said, padding across the room on socked feet, the two beams wobbling. "Here ya go."

Goodness, this kid was working his way into her heart.

Micah clicked on a battery-operated lantern and set it on the coffee table. He cleared away a throw pillow before joining her. "Let's sit here and re-group. You okay there Benji?"

"Yep," the boy said, wriggling to sit in between them. "What are we gonna do if it gets cold? How will we eat supper if we can't turn on the stove? Is my ice cream going to melt?"

Chuckling, Micah hauled him closer. "One question at a time. Based on the weather report, I don't think we're going to get power back any-time soon."

"How come?" Benji asked.

"Well," Micah continued, "the rain isn't going to let up for hours. The roads would be muddy and treacherous for repair crews to fix them."

"How do you know?" Benji was sure full of questions tonight.

Susanna angled forward, keeping her gaze off Micah's strong jaw peppered with a five-o'clock shadow. "Benji, your uncle is a contractor. I would bet he's an expert on things like how weather con-ditions affect working outdoors. If he says the roads are unsafe, I believe him."

Nodding, Benji tugged his long sleeves over his hands as he turned to Micah. "Does that mean Miss Levine's spending the night?"

Susanna struggled to keep her face neutral. Showing surprise would only make the situation more awkward.

Micah cleared his throat. "Let's not get ahead of ourselves. Supper first. Given the lack of power, this is going to be a PBJ night."

As he stretched his arm along the back of the sofa, his hand rested on Susanna's shoulder.

She froze other than chewing on her bottom lip for a charged moment before she shot to her feet. "What can I do to help?"

Benji grabbed his flashlight. "Can I watch my tablet while you guys cook?"

Micah scratched the back of his neck. "What do you think, Susanna? I'm torn. Benji doesn't normally get screen time until after dinner."

She was touched that he asked for her input. "Well, these are far-from-normal circumstances."

He mouthed the word *thanks* and then looked past her. "Sure, buddy, but only while we're cooking. No screens afterward. We'll, uh—" he looked at Susanna, his blue eyes catching in the pale beam of the flashlight "—we'll read books together."

With a cheer, Benji was already charging up the loft ladder with his flashlight. Moments later, the sound of his favorite cartoon drifted down.

Angling to look at the ladder, she swept a strand of hair from her face. "How does Benji do with not having the puppy go up to his room with him?"

"The shelter's adoption counselor really stressed the importance of never leaving them alone together. This makes it easier."

"I'm glad they're careful. I heard of a newly released book about adding a new pet to the family. I should see if they've heard of it." She toyed with the cuff of her shirt with nervous energy, knowing she was babbling but unable to stop her restlessness.

Susanna padded across the floor to check on the dogs and found them curled up asleep together on the dog bed in front of the slate fireplace, low flames crackling and chasing away the chill of the rainy night. Standing outside the glow of the lantern, she allowed herself a moment to just watch Micah, his movements slow and deliberate, pulling down plates, creamy peanut butter and bread.

Micah set his glowing lantern on the counter and opened the fridge, gathering up raspberry jelly, a carton of milk and two bottles of water from the darkness. He grabbed a glass from the open-air shelves, pouring milk into the glass for Benji.

He offered her a bottled water. When Susanna went to retrieve it, her fingers brushed his, heat rising in her cheeks. She was glad for the cover of darkness.

"Thank you." She twisted the cap off, hoping to divert herself from thoughts of the handsome man beside her. "What was your favorite book as a child?"

"I wasn't much of a reader." Micah angled a sheepish look her way. "I know. That's blasphemy to a librarian."

"Well, it's not music to my ears," she said with a dry laugh, taking a swig of her water. "What did your parents read to you?"

"They, uh, well, my grandmother read *Peter Pan* to me when I was in kindergarten." He toyed with the cap of his plastic bottle.

His grandmother? Susanna found her attention jumping from the literary reveals to the movement of his fingers and back again. "Your parents didn't read to you?"

As soon as she said it, she hated the judgmental tone that had crept into her voice. As an educator, she should know better. She busied her hands, unscrewing the jelly jar and dipping the knife. Lifting the blade, she scooped some raspberry jelly out and started to spread it along the slice of bread.

"They worked late. It wasn't like they neglected me." A tic started in the corner of his eye. "I spent a lot of time with my grandparents."

"Grandparents are a wonderful gift." She tried for a benign, nonjudgmental answer, but it was hard for her to understand parents who had so little time for their kids. Even her parents, who'd been so deeply strapped for money, found ways to make her feel like a cherished part of their lives.

"I'm not complaining," he said dismissively, spooning out a liberal scoop of peanut butter. "My parents took care of me. They tried to care for Benji. I'm not a fan of blaming others."

Placing her knife on the edge of the crisp white plate, she searched the pain in his blue eyes and rested a hand on his arm. "I'm not saying you should."

"But your parents read to you all the time, right?" He covered her hand with his, the rasp of his calloused fingers enticing against her skin. "And I can't help wondering if you're saying this is why Benji doesn't like to read and why I had trouble in school."

Oh no. She hated that her words had been so misunderstood. She pivoted, her knees wobbly, and she pressed palms flat against his chest.

"Really, I'm not passing judgment." Her fingers moved ever so slightly, as if of their own volition. She ached to sway closer, to linger. His chest rose and fell faster under her hands but he stayed silent.

Gathering the remnants of her tattered willpower, she stepped back, grabbing her water and raising the bottle to her lips. She needed more distraction. Fast. "How about I show you a bit about construction."

"How do you mean?" His face scrunched with confusion, abandoning the sandwich, angling his body toward her.

Her heart tugged for this man who'd been shuffled aside to his grandmother at every turn. And not because the parents needed the help, but because they seemed to consistently prioritize other needs over their son's. Then repeating the pattern with their grandson.

He deserved some play in his life, a break from being so responsible.

Inspiration lighting, she scooped up Benji's

superheroes quilt off the back of the sofa. "Have you ever built a magical blanket fort?"

Micah couldn't remember when he'd had as much fun on a construction project.

But then Susanna hadn't been a part of any of the making of any other buildings he'd ever produced.

Waiting for Benji to finish changing into his pajamas, Micah peered inside the blanket fort, electric lantern on the ground casting a hazy glow. They'd eaten their sandwiches in fast order, then built the shelter. She'd promised Benji she would read books to him once he put on his favorite glow-in-the-dark skeleton pj's.

Crossing his arms, he admired the finished structure built from his throw blankets. There were some impressive arches in the blanket fort from the peaks in the sofa and the arrangement of his kitchen bar stools. "Not too shabby."

"I learned long ago to stack the odds in my favor by draping the quilt over the back of the sofa. That reduces the chances of collapse." She knelt to check on the dogs that were resting in their kennels, damp and exhausted after their run in the rain. Thank goodness she kept an extra crate at his place for when she tutored.

"The clothespins are a nice touch." He straightened the edge of the quilt she'd spread on the hardwood floor.

"Trial and error taught me that after trying to tie all four corners to chairs, only to have it cave in the middle. And tossing it over a laundry line just left the whole thing vulnerable to the first big wind."

"All astute observations. There's nothing wrong with a sturdy framework." He tried to envision Susanna as a girl, retreating from the world with books, surrounding herself with drying laundry.

"Now, the inside is where the magic happens." She lifted up the front flap of the makeshift tent, tossing cream-colored throw pillows in. "I used to haul as many pillows and stuffed animals as I could in with me. And the final touch? Christmas lights." She turned on the tiny battery-operated lights strung across the opening.

"Beautiful."

And she was. So pretty in her attention to fun even in the details.

Besides, if he was being honest, he couldn't help but take in her details too. Her slim-cut pants, her tight orange long-sleeved shirt with *BOO* in glittering gold across her chest, drawing his eyes to her curves.

Blushing, she looked away, clearly uncomfortable with the compliment. He thought about reaching for her, touching her silky-soft hair. Indulging himself in a moment of just the two of them, with no baggage.

But he didn't want to risk spooking her.

"So, uh." Susanna cleared her throat, reaching into her book bag and pulling out a pamphlet. "I've been meaning to tell you. Hollie said I could make use of the ranch's activities for Benji. She even gave me a brochure."

"That sounds great by me. We were already using some with the day care and when I could get free, but not nearly as much as Benji requested." He looked around for a place to sit and peruse the flier, but even the dining room chairs were taken up in the making of the fort. He pointed inside. "There's no time like the present to test it out."

Susanna brushed the strand of hair that fell in front of her face as she sat down on the floor, her legs folding. Micah set next to her, inhaling her apple-sweet scent.

Flashlight pointed at the brochure, she started to read aloud. "Pack-tivities. Nature scavenger hunt. Paint your own stepping-stones. Evergreen ID. Fake fossil digging. Wild West adventure."

Her voice trailed off, a palpable silence as she omitted the next activities. Chalk hearts and kindness words on trees for loved ones.

He cleared his throat, pointing to the next item. "Look. It's story time with a pup. That's you."

She lowered the brochure to her lap, cocking her head to the side. "It's more than just some vague notion of dogs making us happy—although that's true too. But in this case, the dog is taught to focus on pressure points, like resting his head on your knee or lying on your feet. Deliberately. Not just by accident."

"Like acupuncture and acupressure?" Above their heads, Micah could hear Benji's feet running from one side of his room to the other. Drawers opening and closing.

"Yes, much like that," she said, enthusiasm sparking from her words and filling the tent with energy. "I work hard to train the dog I work with. And I'm connected with a pet therapy organization to make sure Atlas and I are up to date on training. We also get to network with others. It's incredibly enriching."

"There's more that goes into it than I would

have thought." And he was enjoying seeing her come alive discussing it.

"Plenty of people think any nice dog would be a fit for this, without realizing the nuances."

"Such as?" Scooting farther into the fort, he leaned against the sofa, making room for her to join him.

"That it requires a rock-solid temperament on the dog." She hugged her knees to her chest. "The dog needs to have been exposed to all sorts of people and situations so it doesn't startle. And most importantly, the dog needs to want to do the work."

"Meaning what?" He stretched his arm along the sofa cushions, almost touching her. But not quite. He'd been so careful not to cross any lines. Not to send her running when he needed her help with Benji.

But every day, the temptation hovered in the air all around him like the lingering scent of apples.

With each animated tip of her head, her hair brushed along his hand. Like a whisper on his skin. Tempting.

"Just because a dog is listening and behaving doesn't mean the dog is enjoying himself. And if the dog is being coerced—even subtly out of a need to please his person—that will start to wear on the animal's nerves, stressing, leading to the potential to bark or snap."

"How can you tell that Atlas likes to work?" He toyed with a lock of her hair, testing the softness between his fingers.

"I read his body language. It tells the story as clearly as any words or book."

He wound the lock around his finger and wished he could draw her closer. "Has anyone told you lately that you're amazing?"

"Not lately," she said dryly. "Those parent-teacher conferences can be rough."

"Ouch." He let go of her hair and clapped his hand over his chest. "As if I need a reminder of our inauspicious meeting about Benji's reading. But seriously, you've inspired me to look into some projects I could add here for Benji…and for the ranch."

"That's awesome. Well done. I can't wait to hear what you come up with."

This night felt so good. So easy. So right. He couldn't help but want to see if a repeat would be as good. "I'm hoping you'll give me feedback. Once I get the plans drawn up, perhaps you could stay for supper. I'll even cook something better than peanut butter and jelly sandwiches."

Susanna could hardly believe how fast her resolve had crumbled after just one evening of fort building and PBJs with Micah and Benji.

Thank goodness the boy had clambered down the ladder in his skeleton pajamas for story time and saved her from having to answer the question about future meals together. For now, she just had to get through the rest of this evening.

Closing the fourth storybook of the night, she set it aside and reached for another…only to find that Benji had fallen asleep. She clicked off the flashlight, and the bones pattern on his skeleton pj's glowed a hazy green in the dim light. Micah, a shadowy figure, held a finger to his lips and pointed outside the blanket fort.

Carefully, she crawled out into the living area. A low blaze flickered in the fireplace. The reddish-orange glow glinted along his dark brown hair as he fed another log to the hungry flame.

He moved with the grace of a tiger, strong and silent. So much so, Benji didn't even stir inside the fort. The rain was still coming down in torrential sheets outside, and the power hadn't been restored.

As much as she knew she needed space, there was a peace in knowing leaving wasn't an option right now. She could enjoy this pocket of time with Micah and Benji just a little while longer, guilt free.

Micah smiled, his eyes blue-flame hot. "Thank you for the idea to go over the activities list with Benji. He seemed really excited. Like he didn't even know there's educational value wrapped up in it. When I was his age, I would have done anything to have lessons someplace like this."

"Me too." She settled in front of the fireplace, warming her hands to ward off the chill in the damp air. "My parents didn't have a lot of money. I learned to love the library from a young age. We spent almost the whole summer there. Mom and Dad each took me, depending on who was free to watch me."

"That's really great of them to have made use of all those summer camps." He eased to sit beside her, offering her another bottled water.

"Well, sure. But some days we just hung out.

Mom said it was cheaper than running the air conditioner at home."

His chuckle twined with hers.

"Did you have siblings or were you an only child?" he asked.

"Just me. My parents always said they wanted more but it just wasn't in cards for them financially."

"They obviously did a good job with you."

Susanna tapped the glossy brochure to her temple. "They taught me how to be thrifty right alongside teaching me the power of education."

"You were lucky to have parents that invested so much of their time into bringing you up."

"I was… I still am. They're retired, living in a condo in Florida." She inhaled the scent of smoke and flame and man. "What about your family?"

"My parents didn't teach us much about being thrifty, that's for sure." His throat moved in a slow swallow. "They tossed money around like it was water. Vacations. Cars. Expensive dinners. Whatever we asked for, they made it happen. They cared, but…"

Her hand drifted to his knee. "I'm listening."

His hand rested on top of hers, like he was

grounding himself. "My brother was the poster child for spoiled and wild with too much money. He got heavy into the drug scene. He and Benji's mom? They got high together, burned through money. Then she got pregnant."

She could see the weight of that time pressing on him. She linked her fingers with his and squeezed. "With Benji?"

"Yeah." The word came out all gravelly. "Mom and Dad put them both in rehab. And then again. Benji was born prematurely. His detox was... rough."

Stifling a gasp, she held herself stone-still, afraid any movement would stop him from sharing. What a scary time for Micah and his family.

His thumb moved along the inside of her wrist, his gaze tracking the movement as he continued to speak. "A year later, they were back in rehab and moved in with Mom and Dad. My parents tried. They really did. But when Benjamin and Lola left that time..."

"You stepped in to take custody of Benji." Of course he did. She'd known the basics of their situation and how he'd come into the picture. But this? It was beyond anything she'd imagined.

"It's torn the family up," he said softly, his voice weary. "Benjamin and Lola can only see Benji if they complete treatment, and even then, any visitation has to be supervised by child services. Mom and Dad think it's embarrassing and that I shouldn't have dragged the family name through the mud in court."

As if reputation was more important than their grandson's well-being? As if Benjamin and Lola hadn't already hauled their family through the worst of times? She wanted to hug both Micah and Benji tight. They were the innocent victims.

Right after she chewed out Micah's parents. "Thank goodness you were able to be there for him. I don't even want to think about what would have happened to him otherwise."

"I'm not the best for the job, but I'm here. And I'm trying." He pulled his hand from hers, then forked his fingers through his hair. "I keep hoping that will count for something with Benji."

"That counts for a lot." She cupped either side of his face, wishing she could cool the hurt and pain in him. "That counts for everything."

He clasped her wrists in his hands, resting his forehead against hers. Taking comfort, yes. But there was something more too. His ragged breath mixed with hers in the space between them and she didn't want to pull away. If anything, she wanted to move nearer.

And as soon as that thought was born, he moved toward her. All the encouragement she needed to close the distance to meet his kiss.

Chapter Eight

Micah wasn't sure who moved first to initiate the kiss. Him. Or Susanna.

Either way, he was all in.

Palming her back, he drew her closer, slanting his mouth over hers. Tasting the fruity sweetness of jelly from their simple supper.

As far as kisses went, this one was pretty mild because of the sleeping child on the other side of the blanket tent. Yet, even this subtle press of their bodies set his blood on fire, all the more alluring because it was such a simple touch. What more might he feel in a moment of unrestrained passion with her? The way she wrapped her arms around his neck, anchoring him to her, echoed that she felt the same.

A rustle inside the tent pierced through the desire and brought him back to his senses. A quick glance into the makeshift fort reassured him that Benji still slept.

Heart slugging in his chest, he angled back and took in Susanna's wide eyes, the rapid rise and fall of her chest. The gold glitter *BOO* across her T-shirt shimmered with each ragged breath.

Her fingers gravitated to her lips, hovering there for an instant. "That can't happen again."

Those brown eyes of hers smoldering—a living compilation of caution and interest.

Really? He couldn't think of anything other than planning a time for a repeat. "And why would that be?"

"Because I'm Benji's tutor." Her words tumbled out faster and faster in a panicked tangle. "And you're his guardian...his father."

She hugged her arms around her chest, the red glow of the crackling fire highlighting the tight press of her lips as she gathered herself. He ached to kiss her again, to touch her, learn the curves and landscape of her. Susanna swallowed, looking up at him with something he couldn't name darkening her eyes.

"What's really going on here?" He reached for her arm, already anticipating the soft give of her flesh.

Rain still beat on the roof. While it wasn't as strong as before, still it echoed with a brisk sound that matched his own increasingly beating heart as he tried to make sense of this moment.

Cool light from the electric lantern cut through the warm orange glow. Micah could make out her reflection in the mirror, the way she worried her bottom lip.

She shot to her feet and charged to the window. "It looks better outside."

Standing, he leaned against the island separating the kitchen from the rest of the living area. "You don't have to answer my question."

Her back to him, she stayed silent so long that he thought she might take him up on the offer to ignore the question. Then she pressed her palm to the window, her shoulders lifting and lowering with a heavy sigh.

"At my prior school, I dated the father of one of my students. A serious relationship." She paused for a moment, her fingers tracing along the rain-streaked pane. "It didn't end well between us, which caused a lot of…conflict for me at work."

He resisted the urge to cross to her, sensing that would only shut down the conversation. "What kind of conflict?"

"I wasn't fired. They had no cause. I hadn't broken any rules and my job performance reports were spotless." A dry chuckle drifted over her shoulder. The deluge continued outside while the fire crackled indoors. "But the family was wealthy. The grandmother wanted her grandson to marry someone else and saw me as a threat to her plans. She was a big donor and she threatened to cancel a sizable contribution. I decided it was in the best interests of the rest of the students that I resign."

Anger surged inside him, along with a kick of protectiveness. How dare they treat her that way? "That's not right. On so many levels."

"It worked out for the best." She turned to face him again, tugging her shirt in place, smoothing wrinkles from her checkered pants, all signs of restoring order to her world. "This job came open in the perfect place to heal. I'm not giving that up."

A spark lit her eyes, a mix of defiance and pain. And the last thing he wanted was to add even an iota more. "Heard and understood."

She didn't move, as if there might be something more she wanted to add.

Finally, with a small smile, she stepped back. "Thank you. I uh, think the rain sounds like it's easing up. I really should go home."

"Of course. Be careful though." He glanced between her and the window.

"Always." She gathered up her bag, such a contrast of delicate and fierce. Vulnerable and utterly independent. "I hope your power's restored soon."

He worried about her on the road in this weather, especially when she seemed so upset. But he had no claim to her or her decisions. Still, he gave one last effort at looking out for her. "Let me know when you're home safely?"

"I'll text," she said succinctly, hitching her bag onto her shoulder. "Thank you for dinner."

He couldn't miss her boundary there, in her refusal to call. And he couldn't blame her. He'd crossed a line he hadn't known was there with her, and she was pushing back.

Understandable, yes.

But he did regret how very quiet his place seemed once she and little Atlas walked out the front door.

* * *

Susanna wondered why a week of distance since that rainy-night kiss hadn't given her near the objectivity she'd hoped for. That simple kiss still tormented her dreams, leaving her restless in her bed.

Now, driving her little compact sedan with Benji in a car seat in the back drumming his feet in time with the country tune, she couldn't get the echo of Micah's voice out of her head. While she'd been helping Benji with his spelling homework, Micah had left her a voice mail.

Could you bring Benji to me? I don't want to keep you any later today. I'm finishing up a project at the campgrounds.

The rich timbre of his tone had stroked her ear. Tingled through her veins.

She'd done her best to keep her distance, hitting the road the second Micah got home from work each night. She'd only seen him once without Benji. They'd met with the boy's teacher to review the initial testing for a learning disability. The results had merely indicated that his progress would be closely monitored for the next two months, that he could receive additional pullout help in school, and that they would reassess in eight weeks. All data would be sent to Benji's new school since a move was expected after Christmas.

As if Susanna had needed even more of a reminder as to why she should steer clear of Micah Fuller. Bottom line, even if Benji hadn't been one of her students, she still wasn't interested in starting a relationship with a man planning to move. She was ready to put down roots.

Susanna guided her car along the curves of the road, surprised at the ways the landscape was changing. More than just how the leaves had tumbled to the ground.

The progress over the last week at the campground was remarkable.

No longer a rugged patch of woods full of orange and red trees with suggestions of buildings. The tree line had been cleaned up, shaped to contour around the individual sites. And the scaffolding had come down from around the buildings, revealing architecture that matched the Top Dog Dude Ranch cabins.

She eased her car into the parking area and cut the engine, bracing herself to see Micah again, still rattled by the phantom memory of his lips against hers. One deep breath at a time, she calmed herself with thoughts of *Anne of Green Gables*… "Tomorrow is a new day with no mistakes in it…yet."

How she needed that to be true.

Stepping out of the car, bitter autumn wind whipped her hair, nearly tugging her scarf from her neck. Benji shielded his eyes and scurried toward her, kicking pine cones.

"Hey," Micah's voice carried on the breeze. "Over this way."

She searched the grounds and found him waving from the far side by a ring of tree stumps. Just a simple look took her breath away. His broad shoulders and muscular chest. His thick, black hair calling to her fingers to smooth down the cowlick forcing a lock over his forehead. Why did he have to be so enticing? So mouthwateringly handsome in khaki work pants and a heavy flannel shirt?

Taking Benji by the hand, she led him through the construction zone. His sweet little grip reminded her of the importance of this tutoring job. In a short time, he'd worked his way into her heart. She needed to do her best by this towheaded charmer.

Boots crunching sticks and leaves, they approached Micah, who was bent over a tree stump. He had a hammer tucked in his pocket as he made some adjustments on...

A handcrafted fairy house. Three of them.

How. Very. Precious.

She was speechless.

With wooden slats cut into shingles for the roof. Scraps had been used to make doors and window frames. Bits of iron had been welded and bent in balconies, porches and tiny fences. Each house was a little different from the other. Each so charming.

How had she ever thought for a second this man hadn't been trying hard enough with his nephew? Her chest tightened at the visible proof of his thoughtful attempts to connect with the boy.

"Wow," Benji said softly, dropping to his knees in front of the first stump. "It's a home for fairies."

Winking, Micah said, "You should check and see if the fairies left a treat for you."

Susanna's heart gave another rough squeeze.

Benji looked up at him, blue eyes as bright as the clear mountain sky. "You're teasing me."

"Look around and see."

Pulling his hands out of his jacket, Benji began to investigate the perimeter of the fairy homes. Moving aside sticks. Even digging into a pile of leaves.

Finally, he struck gold by peeking into the back of one of the roofs, which sported a little hinged door. Inside, he discovered a sealed bag of lollipops.

"Whoa!" Benji cheered, wiping his hands on his jeans. "Candy. Lots of it so I can share with Ivy." He peeled the wrapper off one sucker and stuck it in the corner of his mouth before stuffing the rest of lollipops in his jacket.

Susanna exchanged a look of pride with Micah. What a generous boy.

"Keep looking, champ." Micah gave an encouraging wave. "I bet there's something else."

Benji's eyes narrowed as, squinting, he resumed the search. Moving around the tree stump, he looked and looked, to no avail. Until finally, he slowed in front of a small toolbox, shiny and new. He glanced over at his uncle, questioning. Micah nodded and waved for him to proceed. Kneeling, Benji opened the latch, lifted the lid and uncovered...a treasure trove of figurines.

Dropping to his bottom to sit, Benji excitedly pulled out tiny gnomes, fairies and winged creatures. "Check it out. There are five fairies and seven gnomes. And dragons and unicorns. I can't wait to show this to Ivy. Uncle Micah, can she come play here too?"

"We can ask her mom."

His cheeks flushed red from the wind, Benji placed the figures up around the stump houses.

"Do you think the fairies would bring her treats too?"

Micah chuckled. "I'll leave them a note."

Benji eyed the cubby in the back of the roof where he'd found the lollipops. "Do they leave candy every time?"

Micah looked her way, his eyes asking her for a way out of the corner he'd boxed himself in.

For Benji's benefit—not because she was tugged by Micah's deep blue eyes—Susannah said, "The fairies only bring treats when the leaves are shaking."

Benji looked thoughtfully at the tree. "I think they're shaking now."

Rich laughter poured from Micah, his love for his nephew shining from his eyes. Their bond unmistakable. "Benji, you inspired all of this."

"Me?" Benji said, sucker stick dangling from the corner of his lips. "How?"

"Absolutely. I thought about that day we went riding and you spun a fairy tale."

Benji pulled the lollipop from his mouth, twirling it between his hands. "With your help and Miss Levine's."

"Yes, a team effort, with you as the leader, kiddo." He ruffled Benji's sun-blond hair before moving around the fairy home. "I was looking at the tree stumps clustered together in this area. Rather than grinding them up, I decided to turn them into artwork so that other children would be inspired to create stories of their own."

"Because kids are going to be camping here?"

"Yes, sir. That's what the campground is about."

Micah's insightfulness and creativity touched her heart, adding new dimensions to her perception of him. She saw the campground through fresh eyes, envisioning the dream vacation he was creating for people on a budget. What she would have given to come to a place like this. Her mom would have helped her make the most of every activity from sunup to bedtime.

Benji took the green, serpentine dragon and put it atop the roof of the first stump home. On the second, he placed two dragons that looked like twins, arranging them as if they were in conversation. "Can we go camping here? All three of us in a tent like we made when it stormed?"

Awareness crackled in the air at the reminder of that night. Her lips tingled like the kiss had only happened seconds ago. Her body hummed with a need for another in spite of all the reasons she needed to run. Run. Run.

Thank goodness Micah kept his composure better than she had managed. He squeezed his nephew's shoulder. "I feel sure we can make that happen."

Benji's smile shined brighter than the afternoon sun beaming though the trees. "And can Miss Levine come with us?"

Whoa. Talk about awkward. Micah still hadn't figured out an answer to Benji's big camping extravaganza. With Susanna?

If only they could go back to questions about fairies leaving treats in trees.

Once again, Susanna had come to the rescue by telling Benji he deserved a camping trip with just his uncle. He stole a glance at her as they walked from the fairy homes. Wind whipping her long rust-colored cotton dress, exposing her matching tights. She pulled the jean jacket closer, her black cat pin glinting in the fading afternoon light. She looked vaguely like a fairy herself. Her gestures and kindness certainly enchanted him.

They picked their way back to her car, careful to stay away from the construction supplies. Little toolbox packed with figurines in hand, Benji skipped ahead, full of boundless energy born of joy and lollipop sugar.

Once Benji had bolted out of earshot but still within eyesight, Micah angled his head toward her. "I'm sorry for what Benji said—about coming camping with us," he said, trying to ignore how they walked shoulder to shoulder, so close he could feel the heat of her, catch the spicy-sweet apple scent of her shampoo. "I promise I didn't prompt him."

"I know that." She skimmed her hair behind her ear.

"Thanks. I wouldn't want you think to think I'm the kind of guy to push." He held up a hand to stop her from speaking. "To be clear, I'm interested. Very. But I respect your reasons for shutting that down."

Her shoulders lowered, some of the tension leaving her face. "Thank you. I'm sorry if I've been avoiding you. The last thing I want is for things to be awkward."

"Me too."

Susanna settled farther into her jean jacket as they walked. "I've been wanting to talk to you…"

"Really?" His heart banged in his chest, hope starting to tug his mouth into a grin.

"About Benji." Her voice was prim, her barriers in place.

He tried to hide the disappointment, remembering how fortunate he'd been to land her help in the first place. But was it so wrong of him to wish for more?

"Right. What's going on?" He bent to scoop a stray nail off the ground and tucked it into his jeans pocket. He couldn't count how many times he later heard nails rattling around in his dryer after being forgotten in his work pants. "Did Mrs. Yoder have more information after our last meeting?"

"Nothing new. But I understand your need to gather as much data as possible before you move. So, I've been thinking this week."

"And?" he prompted.

Her face tightened in concentration and concern. "Has Benji's pediatrician ever said anything to you about possible learning disabilities tied into fetal exposure to drugs?"

His gut clutched at the idea. Still, he searched his memory from that time, knowing Benji deserved for him to explore all the avenues for help with the reading problem.

"Mom and Dad took care of his checkups." Although, how thorough had they been if they were struggling with Benjamin and Lola's issues too? "Benji's not due for another until his birthday."

"Your parents didn't say anything about those doctor appointments?" She pivoted slightly, warm brown eyes inquisitive.

And yes, a bit judgmental. But he agreed with her.

"No, they didn't, although my parents were never the type to buy into learning disabilities." Although as soon as the words left his mouth, he heard the wrongness inherent in them. He'd attended enough functions at Benji's school by now to know the prevalence of challenged learners, students with learning differences. Why hadn't he thought to question more deeply into Benji's obstacles?

Now, thinking back to his parents' take on the situation, he continued with a wince, "My dad always said Benji just needed to work harder."

"Well, with all due respect, your father was wrong." Her mouth went tight. "You have to see he's already working hard, too hard."

Defensiveness flared. He was trying too.

"I don't know much about these things. I've always heard boys develop slower than girls, so I just assumed that's why he was still behind."

Shaking her head, she said, "I can understand how you would draw that conclusion. But I really think it's important to dig deeper in case Benji needs more help."

He hated to think he wasn't giving Benji what he needed. Micah scrubbed a hand over his jaw. "What do think is going on with him?"

"We can't be sure without the testing, but I feel strongly that he has some kind of learning disability. The sooner we identify what that is, then it will be easier to tailor a plan to help him."

Frustration churned inside him, along with anger at his brother. At their parents too, for not looking at the issue more carefully. And piling on top of all that, he couldn't ignore the growing anger with himself since he'd taken this on, knowing his parents couldn't handle it.

What had made him think he was better equipped, a single guy who had no experience with kids? "What kind of tests?"

"Well, you could start with a physical, including hearing and eye tests. Then I can recommend private specialists after that…unless you have someone else you would prefer to ask for a second opinion on this."

"I appreciate your help. I wouldn't even know where to start. And even if I did, I trust you, which is the most important thing of all." His brain swirled with adding more to his already packed schedule. Suddenly baking cupcakes at two in the morning didn't sound so overwhelming. "I hate to ask even more of you, but can you do something to speed things along? I'm due to finish up the project there by Thanksgiving, mid December at the latest, and we'll be moving during the Christmas break."

"We may have the results, or at least some, but you'll have to start all over again in working with staff to make accommodations—after they do their review of the data." She stopped at her car, opening the back door so Micah could remove the booster seat.

"I can see why we need to push this through now." He leaned into her car, air freshener dangling from the rearview mirror and pumping vanilla scent into the compact space. He unbuckled Benji's car seat and walked to his truck. Swinging open the cab door.

Susanna drew up alongside him, hugging Benji's book bag against her chest. "I'll do what I can to help, calling them. But a move makes it tougher. Anything you can accomplish beforehand will really help Benji."

"Moves. Plural." He turned back to face her, booster secured. "My job takes me from location to location. I have to go where the next contract takes me."

Away from Susanna.

No matter how much he told himself that was upsetting because of the loss it would be for Benji, Micah knew he would be feeling the sting himself.

For far different reasons.

As she passed over the book bag, the chasm between them seemed to grow. He swallowed, his throat bobbing as he met her brown eyes, took in the way she folded her arms across her chest. The jean jacket bunched in a way that indicated her current stance had less to do with the nip in the air and more to do with concern for Benji.

Sensing the divide expanding still, he realized this was a crummy time to ask her to please not quit, not to leave him to accomplish this all on his own. Benji wasn't her responsibility. And Micah was in no position to start a relationship. He was already treading water as fast as he could to keep himself and Benji afloat in a world changing too much too fast.

But the thought of Susanna walking out filled him with concern and... He wasn't sure how to label the other emotion. He just knew he needed more time with her. "Before you go, I have another question."

The anxiety in her eyes stung him. He hated that he'd made her feel that way. It wasn't fair of him to dump his worries on her, especially when she was already helping beyond measure with Benji's schoolwork and navigating the complicated labyrinth of specialist testing.

Even more important than all that, actually, she brought such joy to the boy's life.

And Micah couldn't do anything to risk Benji's happiness.

She'd made it clear about her reasons for not getting involved. He had to honor that.

So rather than talk about kisses and chemistry, he simply asked, "Will you go trick-or-treating with us?"

Chapter Nine

"I'm so glad you'll be trick-or-treating with us this evening," Hollie said from beside Susanna in the chair, getting her face painted in the ranch's salon and spa.

Eyes closed, Susanna let the makeup artist do her job in creating a face fit for the Queen of the Forest. Thank goodness Micah had assured her they would be making the candy rounds with the O'Brien family. It had saved her having to disappoint Benji with a half-baked excuse to avoid risking another toe-curling kiss with Micah. "Joining your family will be far more fun than passing out candy at my apartment building. Thank you for including me."

At the start of their transformation, their makeup artists Raven and Fay, dressed as ladybugs, had both put on wireless headphones. This, the young women had promised in unison, would give Hollie and Susanna privacy of conversation.

Hollie's cosmetologist—Fay—rolled her tray of supplies closer. Susanna's beautician—Raven—picked up a fluffy shading eye brush and, instinctively, Susanna fluttered her eyes shut.

Once the light pressure from the makeup brush ceased, she took in the dramatic violets and purples on her eyelids. In the reflection, she could see the bustle going on behind her in the ranch's small salon. Guests in costumes were getting finishing touches on their Halloween look. A table was set up with mini muffins, fruit and cider. Gold and white pumpkins tucked into the hair product shelves were draped with glittery spider webs.

With a sidelong glance, Susanna gauged the progress on Hollie's makeup to accompany her Scarecrow costume. Jacob would be dressed as the Tin Man, and they would be walking their dog, Bandit, in a lion suit.

Hollie's hand drifted to rest on her arm. "I love

that you've chosen to be the Queen of the Forest coming to Sulis Springs. You look gorgeous. It was so generous of Micah to splurge on this whole pampering afternoon for both of us. I would have comped him. But he was insistent, including the tip."

"He's a good man," she answered noncommittally. Just the mention of Micah stole some of the lingering mellow vibes from their massage and five-star lunch.

It was thoughtful of him. Especially when she sensed he was stressed about the construction project. And certainly all Benji's tests with the specialists didn't come cheap.

"A handsome man too," Hollie said.

Discussing Micah's looks? Nope. Not going there. "What activities did the children decide on?"

On her other side, Raven returned to her color palettes, choosing a highlighter shadow in a soft shade of pink.

"Benji's with my crew making papier-mâché masks. The class is making their own paste. And also creating the paints from leftover fruits and vegetables," Hollie explained, her voice just carrying over the hum of hair dryers and a young girl squealing at her transformation into a Cheshire cat.

"Well, that's wonderfully eco-friendly and a beautiful mix with your love of the land." Her mind was already spinning with how to work it in with reading a book about recycling. "What's your recipe?"

"We use fruit and veggies that are about ready to be tossed out. Put each through a strainer and for each teaspoon, add five or six teaspoons of powdered sugar. For brown, we dissolve a little bit of instant coffee and use the same ratio with the powdered sugar."

"That's so inventive." She hoped the next place Benji lived would be as well suited for his need for a multisensory approach to learning.

Where would the Fullers go next?

A thought that she had no business even wondering. "I'm amazed at how much you're balancing with such calm—a holiday with family plus ranch business. And finding time to hang out with me to the mix."

And she had to admit, she was glad she'd decided to come, her friendship with Hollie a real treasure. The decision to spend more time with Micah today hadn't been easy though. She'd considered a hundred ways to duck out of trick-or-treating with Benji and Micah. But there was one great big reason she couldn't deny.

Benji wanted her there.

Hopefully, if they stuck with a group, she would be safe from the crazy-strong attraction to his uncle.

Hollie tilted her head up so Fay could shade in her eyelids with a rich chocolate brown. "Actually, there's no ranch business for me today. I took the day off. This is my first Halloween with the children. Jacob and I wouldn't miss it for the world. We intend to cherish every second."

"And you'll be making amazing memories together." She'd heard Hollie had struggled with infertility, and that she was a cancer survivor. Susanna admired her grit, her determination. Her ability to mine joy from every moment. "But I know it's not as simple as taking one day off. How have you juggled such a big change at once?"

"When we discussed adopting the kids, we decided to delegate whatever business tasks we can. We still plan everything, but my administrative assistant, Ashlynn, carries out some of the hands-on day-to-day operations."

"She seems like a gem." She didn't know the

woman well, but from what she'd seen, Ashlynn was a marvel at making organization look effortless.

Susanna lifted her Mason jar of cider, savoring the crisp apple taste with warming notes of cinnamon and nutmeg. She turned to look at her friend as the makeup artist debated between lip colors—a deep berry and a mauve.

"I trust Ashlynn explicitly." Hollie closed her eyes for Fay to attach long false lashes.

Trust was everything. "How did you find her?"

"Her foster sister—Nina Archer—is the co-owner of our satellite location outside of Nashville."

It was hard not to be intimidated by Hollie's assurance. Everything she touched seemed to turn to gold, whereas Susanna felt like she was struggling to rebuild her life and make her student loan payments on time. "The ranch sure is growing everywhere I look."

"Ashlynn is a godsend. I don't know how Jacob and I would have made this adjustment without her." Hollie fluttered her newly fringed eyelashes and winked at herself in the mirror before smiling over at Susanna again. "I know Micah feels the same about your help with Benji."

"I'm just doing my job." And she would do well to remember that rather than repeat her mistakes.

Instead, she spent a lot of time remembering what it had been like to kiss him. The taste of him simmered through her mind.

"I can tell you've put your heart into that job though. That's making all the difference in the world for Benji."

The pride that she took in the boy's progress made her savor Hollie's praise all the more.

"I would be lying if I said he hasn't stolen a piece of my heart."

"And his uncle?" Hollie pressed, glancing sidelong at her. "Has he stolen a piece of your heart too?"

Her stomach flipped. She struggled not to wince and risk messing up her makeup. She needed to nip this kind of talk in the bud once and for all. "I meant what I said last month. I won't get involved with the parent or guardian of one of my students. That's even truer now that I'm Benji's tutor and not just his school librarian."

Hollie nodded, sweeping off the smock draped over her costume. "I'm sorry for prying." Her face was full of remorse, all heart, just like the scarecrow. "It's really none of my business. Consider the subject officially off-limits."

Off-limits—just like Micah Fuller.

And even as the thought whispered through her mind, another followed reminding her she hadn't chosen to be a funny scarecrow or some other character in baggy clothes.

In spite of how prohibited her employer needed to be, somehow she'd chosen an enchanting gown for a character destined to draw Micah's attention.

"Are you the Hulk or the Jolly Green Giant?"

Micah heard Jacob call out from beside a covered wagon, part of the Halloween display—which was also the designated spot for him and Jacob to meet up with the ladies after they gathered the kids.

Trying not to be insulted at the diss to his costume, Micah looked down at his green hands and emerald-colored sweat suit. He sidestepped a family dressed as vampires and a group of kids with glow sticks. Finally, he reached Tin Man Jacob.

"I'm an alien. There's a mask in my backpack. Benji's an astronaut." He leaned against the side of the wagon, out of the trick-or-treat traffic. "And given you're wearing a tin can, I wouldn't think you've got room to make fun."

"I'm a part of the *Wizard of Oz* trio." Jacob spun around to give Micah the full effect of his metallic outfit.

"Missing a brain?" he asked dryly while waiting for Susanna and Hollie to meet them outside with the children.

The moon had risen high in the sky, a perfect Halloween accessory to the mild evening weather.

"What put you in a bad mood?" Jacob elbowed him good-naturedly. "Did you and Susanna have a lover's spat?"

"I apologize. The paint itches." And holidays reminded him of growing up, making all the memories…with a nanny or the housekeeper. "And Susanna and I are not lovers."

Not in any sense.

An upbeat song about monsters in love pumped through the ranch's loudspeaker. Energy sparked in the room as scores of costumed people meandered past. All the paint and clever costumes made the ranch guests unrecognizable. Micah, who had a knack for remembering faces, found himself unable to fully guess who was whom. A family of mummies passed. A Cheshire cat and caterpillar dog whizzed by, laughter following in the air like a boat wake.

Jacob adjusted his big silver funnel hat. "I'm stepping on conversational land mines all over everywhere. I could have sworn the two of you were a couple."

Micah grunted. Eyes flickering to a young couple—a vampire and vampiress—dancing in the sidelines. Joy coated their fanged-lipped smiles, making the fake blood trailing from their lips seem comical.

"Is that code for me to mind my own business? Because that only makes me wonder more." Jacob clapped him on the shoulder. "Seriously, though. Is there anything I can help with?"

Scratching along the back of his neck and knowing it had nothing to do with the paint, Micah admitted, "She's not interested."

"And you are?" Jacob stepped closer, fixing him with a contemplative stare.

"I've got my hands full taking care of Benji. We're still waiting on test results."

"You haven't heard anything?"

"The eye exam and hearing test showed no issues." Frustration built in him yet again. No matter how often he was told to be patient, that results took time, he was tired of waiting, desperate for answers. "Benji's physical was clear too. The results regarding learning disabilities will take longer."

"I could have sworn Hollie told me the school wouldn't test until he's older, at least another year."

"I paid out of pocket for a private evaluator." Not easy to make happen, but he hadn't seen another way to get things taken care of before their next move.

Jacob gave a low whistle. "That couldn't have been cheap."

He'd briefly considered calling his parents. They'd offered financial assistance often enough. But in the end, he couldn't bring himself to ask. Benji was his responsibility. He'd talked the testers into a payment plan. "It's what he needed. I made it work."

"You're a good dad to Benji." Jacob nodded to a tall wizard in dark robes who waved around a narrow wand as he passed through the growing crowd.

"I'm trying. I came to this gig late." And lately it had been harder than ever with his brother leaving messages that he wanted to see Benji. But there was still a court order in place. If Micah broke that, he would put his own bid for custody at risk.

"You're doing an admirable job. And, from what I've seen, much better than his bio dad and your folks." Micah looked past Jacob to where a staff member dressed as a seahorse handed out candy from the hay wagon. A small line of children began to form, clutching their pumpkin-shaped buckets.

"That's not a high bar." They'd failed Benji again and again. Micah regretted that he hadn't seen the signs sooner and stepped in earlier.

He'd given a lot of thought to what Susanna said about the lasting obstacles Benji might be facing because of drug exposure. And to the fact that Benji's struggles hadn't been noticed with all his parents' drama. That hadn't been fair to the boy, and Micah intended to do whatever he could to give him the help he deserved.

"I'm sorry. That was rude of me. I imagine this has been rough for you, having your family torn apart."

Micah inhaled sharply, the cold flooding his lungs. "No need to apologize. If anyone owes an apology, my brother should say he's sorry for doing drugs around his toddler son."

The words came out bitter, burning his throat, hurting his heart.

"Well, please just know Hollie and I care for Benji. It's hard not to be indignant on his behalf."

Benji may have been short-changed in the past, but he sure had some incredible people in his corner now. "How did you manage to bring in four kids at once as a first-time dad?"

Beyond them, a herd of kids all dressed as jungle animals sprinted from the pumpkin painting booth to the candy apple tent. Excitement animated their footsteps and their laughter carved into Micah's heart. He wanted Benji to have that kind of childhood. He would do anything to make that happen.

"Actually." Jacob paused, his throat bobbing in a slow swallow. "Hollie and I had a son."

Stunned, Micah straightened. "Oh man, I didn't know."

"We adopted a baby boy—JJ." Jacob scrubbed a hand over his chest, right over his heart. "His birth mother changed her mind."

"Wow, that's rough." He didn't know what he would do if his brother suddenly fought to get Benji back.

While he wanted his brother to get his life together, Micah didn't know what it would take for him to trust Benjamin again. Especially when it came to Benji. He wondered what Jacob would advise, because Micah sure could use some insight on this one.

But before he could form the question, his nephew's laughter carried over the crowd. Micah scanned the shifting clusters of kids until he found his little astronaut, recognizing the costume they'd built together out of materials from the work site—such as white hoses and tubes, a two-liter bottle for an oxygen tank.

The O'Brien siblings skipped alongside him, scarecrow Hollie behind them. And beside her...

Micah's heart stuttered at the sight of Susanna dressed as a fairy-tale queen. A silky green gown was gathered at the waist with a gold cord, a flowing emerald cape draped over her shoulders. With her hair piled on top of her head, her rhinestone crown had leaves woven through. Glitter sparkled along her cheeks, her scepter lighting the way.

She was so beautiful she took his breath away. And not just because of the costume, but because it reminded him of that day in the library when she'd told the children the Queen of the Forest legend, spinning a world full of imagination and miracles. A world where healing was possible.

Except she'd made it very clear, her world could not include him.

* * *

Benji poured out his candy on the patio floor, certain this was the best Halloween ever. And it wasn't over.

Uncle Micah had agreed to let them come over to the O'Briens' pretty garden for hot cocoa. Miss Levine had even stuck around too. She looked so pretty in her Queen of the Forest getup. Benji wondered if his uncle noticed. He hoped so.

It would be nice to have a regular family like Ivy did, with a mom who made hot chocolate and went all out with decorations. He felt kinda guilty for thinking that, given how hard Uncle Micah had worked on making their outfits together.

Benji looked down at his astronaut costume, a small smile tugging at his insides. Uncle Micah wasn't too bad at making costumes. Not as good as he was at making buildings, but that was okay.

Still, the O'Briens' garden space was full of fun decorations, spooky, but not in a super-scary way. Cobwebs were draped over the bushes. Lights shaped like ghosts hung from the trees.

While the grown-ups sat around the firepit after changing into regular clothes, Ivy's brothers were trading candy bars. The twins had dressed up as dinosaurs and their older brother as a shark.

Ivy sat beside him, sifting through the contents of her plastic pumpkin. And her costume was the coolest—a spider holding a stuffed pig named Wilbur.

Not surprising she picked a storybook character.

"Benji, you can have this." Ivy passed over a plastic egg with green goop coming out. "This feels slimy."

"And gooey. Which is cool." He extended his hand.

"And messy." She scrunched her nose, dropping the candy into his palm. "Do you have any Snickers bars to trade?"

Benji's mouth dried up. "That's the one in the brown wrapper, right?"

Except there were a lot of brown wrappers in the pile.

"It starts with an S. It looks like this." She traced her finger in the dust on the patio tile. "Sssss. Ssss. Sound the word out."

"I'm trying." He knew she was trying to be nice and help. But he hated feeling like a baby. He grabbed the closest piece of candy in brown wrapping. "Here you go."

"That's a Milky Way bar." She nudged it back.

"That goes with your astronaut costume though. I'll just find the Snickers myself."

She pointed. And he wouldn't have been able to tell the letters anyway because his eyes were stinging with tears. He wanted the ground to open up like a black hole in the galaxy and swallow him right up.

It had been bad enough when he threw up during the cookie making. But he wasn't gonna cry. And he wasn't going to puke.

He was getting out of here.

Grabbing the pillowcase he'd used for candy, he raked his haul back in. "Uncle Micah, I'm ready to go."

He stumbled to his feet, his bag swinging.

"Careful, buddy," his uncle called out an instant before the pillowcase thudded against something.

Behind him, Ivy squealed.

The grown-ups gasped.

Stealing a look backward, Benji saw he'd hit her in the head with his sack full of candy. Tears streaked down her face. Her parents leaped up, followed by Uncle Micah and Miss Levine.

Benji froze, feeling all panicky and afraid. And he wasn't sure exactly why other than knowing that good people didn't hurt others. The grown-ups were gonna be mad at him. Uncle Micah would be angry at him.

And he'd have to move. Again.

Without thinking, he hugged his bag to his stomach and ran out of the garden. Fast. Feet pumping as he bolted through the archway that led out. A spiderweb decoration caught him in the face and he smacked it away just as he bumped into someone.

"Careful there," the man said in a voice that sounded just like Uncle Micah.

Except it wasn't.

A weird, sick feeling made him wonder if he'd puke after all tonight.

Because Benji looked up to see his dad standing over him. And somehow he knew there was something a whole lot worse than moving. He might be taken away.

Chapter Ten

At the sound of Ivy's cry, Susanna pivoted fast in her seat at the firepit. She found Ivy sitting in the middle of a pile of Halloween candy, holding her shoulder while Benji backpedaled away, the pillowcase full of treats clutched in his fist. His words and Ivy's were swallowed by revelry from the ranch's festival, applause and cheers, music and laughter.

Back in the secluded patio, big fat tears streamed down Ivy's face, strings of lights overhead whipped to and fro by the night wind. Hollie and Jacob shot to their feet and ran to their daughter, kneeling. Susanna crossed quickly, joining Micah to hover nearby while the parents comforted their child.

Hollie kissed her fingers and pressed them to Ivy's shoulder. "All better?"

Gulping, Ivy nodded, rubbing her shoulder, the extra spider legs on her costume moving in sync. "Benji didn't mean to thunk me with his sack. Don't be mad at him."

Susanna looked around the patio, seeing the dinosaur twins huddled over their buckets of loot. In the soft glow of the firepit she could see Freddy the shark was curled up on the lounger, half-asleep.

A cold knot of dread gelled in her gut. "Micah, where's Benji?"

"I just saw him. He's right over…" He stopped short. His face went tight with alarm. "Benji? Benji, where are you?"

No answer came. Just the echo of hoedown music in the distance along with cheers beyond the patio's tree line. Benji knew better than to wander off, especially at night. But if he had, on a night such as this, she didn't even want to consider how hard it would be to find him in the crush of costumed people.

Or how easy for someone to snatch him.

Her stomach plummeted like rocks slipping beneath the surface of a calm lake. She knew she needed to stay clearheaded and calm. Giving in to the panic wouldn't help find Benji. But as her gaze scanned the party, searching for any sign of the boy, the sea of kids in masks didn't yield any clues.

Who would have thought there were so many astronauts trick-or-treating?

"Jacob," Micah said, concern creeping into his voice as he fished for his phone, then activated the flashlight. "Hollie? Do you see my nephew?"

Hollie rocked back on her heels, looking around and then back to her daughter. "Ivy, honey, where's Benji?"

Ivy's jaw trembled. "But it was an accident. Don't be mad at him."

"Okay, sweetie, I hear you. We're not angry." Hollie's voice rose ever so slightly, but unmistakably, with worry. "But where is Benji? We need to find him."

She swiped away her tears with her sleeve, then pointed toward the arbor. "He went that way. I think. But I wasn't watching real close. I'm sorry."

Just beyond the archway covered in lights, the gate gaped wide open. He could be anywhere on the property by now. Susanna sucked in a deep breath, trying to steady herself and think of where Benji was most likely to wander off to.

Micah sprinted toward the arbor with Susanna close on his heels.

"You go left," he said. "I'll go right. We'll text if we find him."

"Got it."

She'd barely made it three steps when Micah's voice, hissing a low curse, stopped her short.

"Benjamin?" Micah's tone iced the night air. "What are you doing with Benji?"

Micah wondered how a perfect evening could turn to garbage so fast.

But then that tended to be the norm where his brother was concerned.

At least Benji was safe. For now.

Finding Benji with Benjamin had been a shock, to say the least. Rather than risk a scene in public, Micah had taken Jacob's suggestion that they return to the private patio area to sort things out.

Guests milled about, passing in front of the arbor gate. Laughter and excited conversation whirred past as Micah strode back toward the O'Briens' patio. It seemed as though a few small steps threatened to upend the peace Micah was trying so hard to build for himself and Benji.

He and Benjamin might look like siblings, with the same hair and eye color, but they couldn't be any less alike on the inside. At least, Micah hoped that was the case.

Assessing his brother for drug use, he checked the whites of his eyes and found them bloodshot and his clothes rumpled. That could be from the long drive, but he doubted it. He knew better than to believe anything Benjamin said when he was under the influence.

Although steaming mad at his brother's deliberate violation of a court order to stay away from his son without supervision, Micah held his tongue for now. He needed to get Benji settled before finding out what Benjamin intended with this latest stunt.

As Micah entered the garden, his heart seized again. The O'Briens' kids fell silent, candy scattered on the ground. Ivy fiddled with the frame of her black glasses, her spider legs moving with the gesture. Her siblings looked on with equal unease, all wide-eyed and taking in everything.

How very embarrassing and wrong that they had to witness this mess.

Micah rested a hand on Benji's shoulder. "Go

on in with Mrs. O'Brien for a minute while I talk to your dad."

"Why do I have to go with Ivy?" he said with a quaver, clutching Micah's hand. His nephew's grip was so tight, his nails pressed into Micah's hand. "I wanna stay here with you, Uncle Micah."

Susanna fluffed her dress out, making it easier for her to kneel at Benji's eye level. "They just need some time to talk. Your father's visit caught everyone by surprise. How about I come inside with you too?"

A gentle smile spread across her face. Benji looked at Micah and then back to Susanna before giving a nod.

Once again, she'd come through for him and his nephew. How could he ever repay her?

And how would they manage after the move?

Hands in his pockets, Benjamin wore jeans, a leather jacket and an easygoing grin that had fooled far too many people. "Don't you want to hang out and see your old man?"

"Uncle Micah?" Benji's bottom lip trembled.

"It's okay, buddy." Micah kept his tone level, for Benji's sake, even though he wanted nothing more than to flatten his brother for being so utterly clueless when it came to the boy's well-being.

"I'll sort this out and then we can decide where to go from there."

Benji hugged his bag of candy close like a security blanket as he peered up at them. "You're not gonna leave me, are you?"

Benjamin scrubbed the back of his neck, that too-easy grin still painted on his face as he said, "Of course not."

Benji shook his head. "I mean Uncle Micah. You won't leave me?"

Micah's heart cracked open. He knelt, cupping his nephew by both shoulders. "I won't leave you. I promise. I'm here for you always."

Susanna extended her hand, and Benji moved quickly to grab it. Hollie quickly herded her children inside, holding the door open for Susanna and Benji. As they moved away from Micah, he heard Susanna offer to tell another fairy tale. Benji shot one last glance over his shoulder before he climbed the steps to the O'Briens' private space.

Thankful he could trust Benji was in safe hands, he turned his attention to his brother, once again studying his eyes, his demeanor, for any signs he might be high or drunk.

Benjamin's eyes followed Susanna, taking her in, something like spite curling his lip into a smile that fell short of pleasant. "Is your girlfriend playing mom to my son? He already has a mother. Lola."

"Susanna's a librarian at his school and his after-school nanny and tutor," he said tightly, standing, watching. On guard. Wondering if Lola was going to pop out from around a corner. Yet knowing that even if he asked Benjamin about her, there was no way to trust the answer.

"A tutor? Wow, you must be doing well, little brother," Benjamin said right as Jacob returned to the patio, staying quietly in the shadows.

While Micah found the whole situation embarrassing, he knew this conversation could get ugly. For Benji's sake, it was best to have a witness to his side of the story.

And backup if Benjamin went off the rails.

His brother didn't look high, but then he'd gotten adept at hiding the signs over the years—after far too much practice avoiding detection.

Jacob gestured to the iron table. "Why don't we all take a seat."

Micah exhaled hard, nodding in agreement. He appreciated his newfound friend's level-headed influence, and he also didn't miss how Jacob sat in the chair closest to the door, making himself a human barrier between Benjamin and the kids.

Micah flattened his palms to the table. "How did you find us this evening?"

Sure, living here wasn't a secret, but they hadn't been at the cabin.

"I told the guy at the registration desk that I'm your brother." Benjamin paused when Jacob's jaw flexed with tension. "Don't be mad at them. I showed my ID. When I explained we're also business partners, they pointed me in this direction."

Micah ground his teeth. "But we're not business partners."

Benjamin shrugged, tapping his fingers in rapid succession on the iron table that spoke of nervous energy. "I didn't come all this way to risk getting turned away."

"What are you doing here?" Micah asked, his patience growing thin.

"I want to see my son," Benjamin said. "It's Halloween. I just wanted to get a look at his costume and give him some candy."

A seemingly innocent claim. Except Micah knew it wasn't that simple. It couldn't be. Not with Benji's well-being at stake.

Enough small talk.

"Benjamin," Micah said sternly, "you know that when Benji was removed from your care, the courts stipulated that all visits had to be conducted in the presence of a social worker. You're in violation of that agreement."

Benjamin leaned back in his chair, putting his hands behind his head with eyebrows raised. "I didn't agree to anything."

Semantics. Micah bit back the urge to knock the legs out from under Benjamin's chair. "I'm not going to argue with you. Let me know where you would like to meet tomorrow, and we can talk. Provided you're clean."

"And you'll come with Benji?"

His brother seemed so hopeful, it almost tugged at Micah's heartstrings.

Almost.

"We'll discuss that tomorrow," Micah stated again. Which would give him time to check into legalities. Micah didn't want to make a misstep that would jeopardize his own custody of Benji. The boy had been through enough.

Micah escorted his brother out, giving himself a beat to sort through what he would say to Benji. The boy would be full of questions Micah couldn't answer. Susanna was always so good at knowing what to say. Hopefully he could muddle through with Benji tonight until he could find time alone with Susanna to pick her brain for direction.

Even though he knew this went far beyond Susanna's job description as Benji's tutor and after-school nanny, Micah couldn't help but be grateful for the day she'd stormed into his life.

The next morning, Susanna wondered if her heart would ever slow down. She'd taken the day off work, unable to wait at school all day. Wondering. Worrying. So she'd charged back to the work site again, like that first day, except this time, they went into the work-site trailer to plow through concerns for Benji.

As she claimed her seat across from Micah, paperwork for Benji spread on his worktable, she was just glad Benji was safe at school. His teacher and the front office had been notified only Micah or Susanna could check him out. Micah had asked for her assistance in organizing data in case child services requested additional documentation on Micah's parenting thus far.

Micah shuffled papers on his worktable. Warm overhead lights cast a slightly yellow hue over the space. A silver bowl was piled high with Halloween candy. Wrappers from sour candies littered the surface.

Last night had ended on a tense note, to say the least. She'd hoped for some answers, but once Benji's biological father left, Micah had gathered up his nephew and bid everyone good-night, using the excuse that it was a school night.

But he wasn't fooling Susanna one bit. She could read him too well after the weeks of getting to know him. He was embarrassed…

And afraid.

Which scared her. She couldn't bear to think Micah's wild-eyed brother might snatch Benji and run off. Things like that happened far too often. She'd just never considered it could happen to a little one in her care.

"Are you okay?" she finally asked, cupping her thermos of coffee. "It had to be tough seeing your brother out of the blue like that."

His jaw flexed. "It was a shocker, for sure."

"For Benji too." Truth be told, she was still rattled. She wished she had Atlas with her, just to hold and breathe. But she'd dropped him at the ranch's doggy day care, unsure about monitoring her dog around the construction equipment.

And she was able to give her entire focus to Micah.

His cheeks puffed with a long exhale. "Benji didn't really talk about it much last night or this morning on the way to school."

"Do you think that's healthy?" she asked gently, thinking Micah would benefit from Atlas's comfort too.

"No. But then none of the way he's landed in my care is healthy. For now, I figured it was best to let Benji call the shots on how and when to talk about his dad."

Susanna crumpled a candy wrapper in her fist, remembering with a pang how worried Benji had been the night before. She'd done her best to comfort him with a story, but she'd seen his distraction. His fears. "I can see the wisdom in that."

Micah's gaze held hers, gratitude shining at her support. "I appreciate your keeping me company. I need to get everything—absolutely everything—in order as far as documents for Benji's schoolwork," he said, shifting papers into folders, adding sticky notes. Satisfied, he set the folders down, and reached for the candy. He popped a bite-sized chocolate into his mouth and added the wrapper to his pile. "I need to prove to the courts I'm doing right by the boy."

Susanna glanced around the construction trailer, her eyes catching on a black-framed photograph of Micah and Benji at two or three. The photograph was arranged next to his sleek desktop computer. Piles of papers were arranged neatly on the edge of his modern, metal desk.

Above the drafting table hung a giant cork-board. Gold thumbtacks pressed into the four corners of a blueprint. To the left of the blueprint was a project schedule.

Slinging her bag onto the table strewn with still-in-progress blueprints for the campground, she pulled out her phone, in case the school needed to reach her. "Do you mind my asking where Benji's mom is?"

"Still in rehab, apparently. Where Benjamin is supposed to be too." Micah grabbed more candy, stress seeming to motivate his mindless munching. Dark shadows spoke of his lack of sleep, fine lines at the corner of his eyes shouted concern. He glanced at a paper on his desk and crumpled it, tossing it onto the overflowing trash can. "I made some calls this morning to Lola and to my attorney and learned that Benjamin checked himself out against doctor's orders. So, now, he can't see Benji at all. It's out of my hands."

"How so?" She hated the helplessness in his voice. Knew he had to be out of his mind waiting for definitive answers.

"According to my attorney, the only way Benjamin and Lola were allowed to keep any visitation was if they completed the treatment program." He took a long drag from his coffee mug. Micah's shoulders sagged as he set the mug on a dragon coaster Benji had made in Susanna's after-school reading group. "He's checking in with child services now to discuss filing the appropriate documents."

"That puts you in an awkward position."

"Not really." He braced his palms on the table so hard his hands turned white. "If I let my brother see Benji, then that puts my custody at risk. And there's not a chance I'll allow that to happen."

His heavy sigh spoke of the grief behind those words, the tug-of-war over being Benji's advocate, while possibly losing his brother in the process. And then, there was Benji, who must be so confused— not to mention hurt—over the tensions in his family.

"Family is complicated." She rested a hand over his, holding firm.

"Not yours." He sank back into his seat. "You're lucky in that."

"I know." And at the same time, realizing that on some level she hadn't known. She'd been too focused on her family's lack of money, rather than all the blessings. But today wasn't about her or her past. "What can I do to help?"

"What you're already doing. Being there for Benji…" His voice broke. He cleared his throat and started again. "And for helping me through all this paperwork so I can make at least one thing in his life easier."

The deep well of pain in Micah's eyes, in every tense line of his big body, tugged at her. Even as he turned his back to her, pinching the bridge of his nose, his shoulders stooped. Regardless of when he would leave Moonlight Ridge, he was here. Now. And he needed someone to comfort him over the betrayal of one family member after another.

Her heart in her throat, Susanna pushed away her chair and walked up behind Micah. Without hesitation, without regrets, she wrapped her arms around his waist and rested her cheek against his back.

As she soaked up the heat of his body against her cheek, breathed in the scent of detergent mixed with his body wash, she wondered how she would manage to gather up all the bricks of her crumbling resolve.

Chapter Eleven

Micah soaked up the feel of Susanna's arms around him, her cheek resting on his shoulder blade. The soft give of her breasts against his back. He'd wanted something like this from the moment they'd kissed.

Sooner than that.

From the instant he'd seen her marching across the work site, full of fire. He wanted to keep on taking the comfort she offered in the middle of his complicated, messy life.

But that would be unfair to her. He had so little to give her in return.

Pivoting in her hug, he indulged in a second to hold her back. Then breathed in the sweet apple fragrance of her shampoo. What would it be like to meet her under normal circumstances, to ask her out on a date?

But he had a child to bring up and bills to pay with a job that necessitated a vagabond existence.

Still, he stroked along her silken hair and said, "I'm sorry, but I'm not in a good place right now, after Benjamin showed up out of the blue."

"It was unsettling, to say the least." She burrowed deeper into his chest, her curves subtle under her long sweater and leggings. Susanna ran a gentle hand down his plaid shirt, her touch soft and enticing.

A sigh of longing racked through him. "There's nothing I want more right now than to kiss you again. I'm holding on to my self-control by the skin of my teeth."

"You're not alone in that," she whispered. "I've dreamed of that moment."

His palms sketched lower, to her waist. His mouth skimming over hers. She leaned closer. He anchored her. Anchored them both into undiluted sensation. The taste of chocolate on her tongue, the silken glide of her hair through his fingers.

The office space afforded them privacy, complete with a room with a daybed for crashing when he worked long hours.

Need cranked higher and hotter in him, a desire for more. And from her response, he could tell the attraction was reciprocal.

But he owed it to her to take a beat. To see where she stood. Even if they were on the same page, he wanted to give her something more romantic, more intentional than a quickie in his messy office.

He eased away, resting his forehead to hers. His breath synced with hers as his hand trailed up to brush a thumb over her lips. He strengthened his resolve even with their hearts hammering in concert. "You've made it clear you aren't interested in pursuing anything serious between us right now."

A wince twitched through her, her eyes staying closed. "I can see how you would want a distraction from all that's going on with your brother and Benji."

What? He cradled her face in his hands. "You're not a distraction. Lady, you're a beautiful temptation." He hoped she heard the raw honesty in his voice. He swallowed. Hard. "You have been from the moment you came charging across the work site with steam coming out of your ears."

Hands crawling upward, she looped her arms around his neck. Susanna looked at him through her long lashes, the warm brown of her eyes threatening to pull him back into that kiss, into the impulse to be closer to her.

A half smile tugged at the corner of her pink mouth. "Funny thing is, I'm not bold. Not by nature. I'm a hyper-responsible bookworm whose idea of self-care is losing myself in the pages of a fat novel."

Her words knocked around in his brain until they settled and he wondered. Had he been taking advantage of her good nature? He hoped not. Because that would be incredibly unfair to the kindest person he'd ever met.

Dragging in a ragged breath, he eased back a step. The apple scent of her shampoo fading. His insides chilling. "I hope you know how much I appreciate all you've done for Benji and for me. The last thing I want is to take advantage."

Confusion shifted through her eyes, along with a whisper of hurt. He felt like a jerk. But it was better this way.

"Oh, uh, right. We both acted impulsively. No

harm, no foul." She smoothed wrinkles from her overlong white tunic. Just like that, the half smile morphed into a curt, no-nonsense line. "Do you still want me to pick up Benji after school?"

"Yes, please. It won't be for much longer," he said, as a reminder to himself as much as to her. "And I'll make sure you're well paid."

Her mouth went tight and she backed toward the door, breaking his heart with her vulnerable eyes. "If you have questions, you know where to find me."

Unlocking the cabin door, Susanna juggled the two dog leashes, Atlas and Jupiter tangling up together. Benji trailed after her, his book bag dragging the ground.

Her head was still spinning from Micah's about-face. She thought they'd developed a...friendship. Okay, not that exactly, but a connection, even if they both had different goals that precluded a relationship.

She just hadn't expected hitting the brick wall of rejection to hurt so much.

Benji slung his book bag onto the table. "Would you mind reading me a book while I eat my after-school snack?"

His request surprised her. He usually preferred to run outside, reading being the last thing on his list of preferred activities.

"Of course. I'm happy to read to you," she said, unhooking the leashes, releasing the pups to race to the water bowl. She shrugged out of her jacket and strode to the pantry.

Opening the door, she picked Benji's favorites, a bit of an unspoken reward for choosing a book. Whatever she could do to make the experience positive. She hip-bumped the cabinet closed again and placed the peanut butter crackers and juice box on the island, Benji scooting up onto the bar stool.

"Thanks," he said, nudging a hardback book toward her. "Here ya go. I picked it out in class today from Mrs. Yoder's library. Not yours. So maybe you haven't read it before."

She spun it to face her, surprised at the pumpkins on the front. She recalled the story, comparing a puppy's scary day to a haunted house adventure, meant to help children empathize with their pets. "But this book is a Halloween book. That's passed."

"I wanna read it now, though. I mean. I want you to read it to me." He peeled open the crackers with careful concentration, not meeting her eyes.

"You know me." She grinned. She tapped her finger to the book cover, head tilting as she tried to understand Benji's suddenly shy demeanor. "I'm always happy to read. What made you choose it?"

Setting the cracker down, Benji looked up at her with wide blue eyes. His little face serious, brow furrowed in something that looked like frustration.

"Well, Mrs. Yoder read it to us and I have some questions. I was afraid if I asked in class, the other kids would make fun of me. I want you to explain it to me. Mrs. Yoder said it's a scary book, but I don't understand why."

Susanna leaned on the countertop. Working with a student who struggled with reading meant that she wanted and needed to lower every barrier. That included any and all judgment.

She refused to be the reason a student cried over a book. "So would you like to discuss the story, rather than just read it?"

He nodded, stabbing the straw in his drink. "Yes, please. If that's okay and not too stupid."

Reaching for the peanut butter crackers, he brought the snack to his mouth. He bit off a corner, chewing thoughtfully.

Stupid? Her breath hitched at the word. She hated when any child thought that about themselves. But with Benji's learning struggles, she worried all the more for his confidence.

And yes, because Benji had a very special place in her heart.

"I think it's wonderful that you want to understand the story better. Reading is about so much more than just the letters and the words. It's about the content." She took her seat beside him, thinking through the story as best she recalled. "So, in answer to your question, the book is scary because it's full of things that would frighten a dog."

"What things are they afraid of? I wouldn't want Jupiter to get scared."

He scooted in his seat to get a better look at his puppy, who was sniffing his boots. Jupiter sneezed, her black ears flapping back. Atlas was curled up in front of the door, watching, his head tipping to the side.

Thumbing open the cover, she flipped to different pages, pointing to images. "Well, some get nervous going to the veterinarian."

"Because they are gonna get a shot? I don't like shots." He wriggled, spinning the stool's swivel top. "But I get a sucker and a sticker after."

"And dogs get a treat afterward too." She skipped ahead to one page after the other, revealing different watercolor illustrations. "There are other things in there like a big vacuum cleaner and fireworks and a washtub."

"But I like baths." He swiped his sleeve across his mouth. "That's kinda dumb, though, right? Phillip and Elliot said they hate baths because then it's bedtime."

There was another self-deprecating word. *Dumb.* Something else was going on here. She just hoped Benji would open up to her, if she was careful and didn't push too hard. "What else would be in the haunted house? Other than something in this book?"

Benji chewed his bottom lip, avoiding her gaze and crumbling a cracker. When he spoke, his voice was small, full of pain. "Scared of being left alone for a really long time?"

What was he getting at?

"There are some dogs who really struggle with that." She reached down to trail her fingers along Jupiter's back as the puppy ambled past.

He picked up the juice box. Took a sip, swallowing slowly. Benji's blue eyes stayed averted, following Jupiter as she made her way to the tan couch.

"Some kids don't like that either." Benji's chin trembled.

And there it was. The reason for choosing this book. Not concern about being teased over reading problems. Rather, this whole conversation was about deeper-rooted fears. "Some kids like you?"

"Sure. Maybe." He picked at the frayed knee of his jeans.

She waited, letting him find his pace. Hoping that Micah would get home soon to be a part of an increasingly important conversation. Because it wasn't her place to bring up the subject of his father's visit.

The moment stretched, silence broken only by the sound of Benji crinkling the cracker wrapper in his fist and dog nails clicking across the floor.

Just when she thought that perhaps he would open up on his own, Benji's face turned red and he looked away, hopping off the bar stool. "I think I hear Uncle Micah coming home."

Even now, with Benji's worries preying on her mind, Susanna's heart stuttered in anticipation over Micah's arrival. Why couldn't she remember that she was the tutor and nanny, and nothing more? Hadn't Micah reminded her of that in no uncertain terms the last time they were together?

Steeling her heart for seeing him, Susanna told herself to keep it together. Be a professional. And she would, because Benji needed her and that was a trust she wouldn't risk.

Micah thumbed the key fob, locking his truck, still feeling like hell after the way he'd handled things with Susanna. He hated that he couldn't have found a better way to explain himself to her.

He was trying. Really trying to put the pieces of his life together and be a better person than his brother, than his parents. He wanted to break the crazy cycle passed down through generations of people who didn't care about the little ones in their life, not in a meaningful way that let a child know their needs came first.

He opened the gate to his cabin, wondering where he would be living once he left this place. On jobs in the past, he'd just found the cheapest studio available. He had a whole different set of priorities and needs now.

Barking carried on the wind, giving him a moment's warning before Atlas and Jupiter came barreling around the corner of the house. Benji ran after them, his coattails flapping.

Susanna was only a few steps behind, the setting sun casting a glow around her. Rays highlighted the warm undertones of her brown hair falling in waves on her white shirt. She was a vision in her oversize shirt with black leggings, booties and a plaid scarf. Effortless beauty that sent him back to their kiss in the construction trailer.

All her things were on the porch steps. Like she didn't even want to go back inside once he arrived. A pang of guilt mixed with regret ricocheted through him as he approached.

Micah waved to her, trying to introduce more ease into the situation than he felt. "Thanks for picking Benji and Jupiter up. I didn't mean to keep you so late."

A tight smile painted her lips. The warmth of her brown eyes seemed to have faded. Tension flexed along her jaw and he hated that he had done anything to put it there in the first place.

"That's what you're paying me for." She cast a glance Benji's way as he ran circles around a tree with the dogs, then she looked back at Micah, and whispered, "Do you have a minute to chat?"

He rubbed a crick growing in his neck. "About earlier?"

"Actually, no." She stuffed her hands in the

pockets of her fleece-lined jacket. "About something that just happened with Benji."

Alarm cranked the crick tighter. "Sure, how about we walk the dogs and talk."

Minutes later, he had the dogs leashed up and Benji's jacket zipped for a trek along the Top Dog Dude Ranch trails.

Weeks ago, this path had been shaded by red-yellow leaves. Now, more branches were bare, haunting. Or maybe that was just his apprehension coloring his perception as they made their way down the trail.

Susanna kept pace with him, watching Benji as he bounded ahead, full of energy as always. Once he was out of earshot, she looked back quickly and cleared her throat. "He wanted to discuss a book that he brought home from school. We were sharing things that dogs are afraid of and he shifted the conversation to things that would scare kids."

Micah wanted to curse his brother all over again for the way he'd shown up out of nowhere. "What did Benji say?"

"It may mean nothing…"

He suspected otherwise, or she wouldn't have mentioned it. "But?"

"In talking about what would scare a child—"

she dipped her head closer to whisper "—he listed 'being alone.'"

The anger at his brother multiplied, sinking roots deep as he realized the source of Benji's worry. "You were right to tell me. Thanks. Please know I would never leave him unattended. He's just a kid."

"I know that. Absolutely." She rested a hand on his sleeve, then pulled back. "You're good with him."

His eyes drifted to Benji who paused up ahead, looking at a pet pig on a bright pink leash. He turned back, blue eyes bright with excitement. Benji pushed his blond hair out of his face, shouting back to them. "It's just like Ivy at Halloween."

"We'll have to tell her all about it," Susanna called, her voice big and bubbly, a stark contrast to her tone a minute ago.

Jupiter pulled on her leash, impatient to catch up with her boy. Moments like this, it was almost easy to forget that Benji's childhood was littered with barriers and rejection. The boy smiling at the pig and its owners, a graying couple in their sixties, had already been through so much disappointment in his short life.

Micah fixed his eyes ahead, willing back the

surge of anger. "His parents used to leave him… in the house…in the car. His day care provider learned about it and contacted the authorities. Once an investigation was launched, the neighbors filled in the details." And he still struggled with how to forgive his brother for the unforgiveable. "That's when he went to live with my parents."

"That explains the book." She pressed her fingers to her lips before adjusting her hold on the leash again. "I hate that he has to carry that trauma inside."

Across the pond, a family gathered for what appeared to be a gender reveal with balloons of blue and pink flanking a young couple. In front of them, there was a box with an elaborate-script question mark. The husband leaned over, lifted the lid of the box. Pink streamers popped out and the family erupted with whoops of excitement as the husband and wife shared a kiss.

So much hope in that moment. Had Benjamin and Lola ever been that genuinely excited about the birth of their child?

"I just wish someone had spoken up sooner." Micah twined and untwined his fingers into the leash loop. "Hell, why didn't I step in sooner?"

She stopped walking, her hand touching his

shoulder again. Fluttering her eyes shut, she took a deep breath. When her eyes reopened, the softness had returned. A forlorn expression parted her lips slightly open before she spoke, searching his eyes.

"As someone in the school system, I can say there's so much we see about our students that we can't always act on because we don't have proof. Things that feel 'off' about a kid's home life. It's hard being the voice for those children and wondering if we should have stepped in earlier." She took his hands. "You don't have to wonder. You did the right thing, more than anyone else has been able to do for Benji."

Her words washed over him like a healing balm and he hadn't realized until then how much guilt he carried around. The longer Benji stayed in his care, the more he grew to love the kid, the worse he felt that he'd been so wrapped up in building his career he hadn't paid closer attention to his family.

Not that he thought he had the power to change them. His parents, Benjamin, Lola, they were all adults.

Benji was a child. And that was the point. "I need to keep doing right by my nephew." A boy he loved like a son. "If I can just get through this contract, I'll have the kind of flexibility I need to be there for him for the rest of his life."

"I'm glad Benji has you now."

He resisted the urge to reach out to her. "I need your help for just a little while longer."

"I made a commitment to Benji for as long as you're here, and I keep my word."

That kind of integrity and character was rare. Rarer than he'd known.

And he couldn't escape the realization that he might be losing far more than he'd expected when he left this place behind.

Chapter Twelve

This day had been complicated and so very long for Susanna. Especially considering that she'd taken time off.

Now, on her return trip to the cabin after her walk with Micah and Benji, her feet hurt.

Her feelings too.

Because she wanted to linger on this stroll with Micah, wished life could be simple for once and they could have more afternoons like this. The draw toward Micah grew too strong to ignore. Different from what she'd felt for anyone before, even with her last relationship. Quickly, she hauled her thoughts off the bad breakup at her last school and focused on the beauty of the day.

Deep sunset colors purpled overhead, light receding as they strode through the tree-covered path back toward Micah's cabin, passing the main lodge, only a stone's throw away. As the sun slunk farther beneath the horizon, the afternoon chill turned more biting. Susanna's breath pooled in front of her face, and she repositioned her plaid scarf.

Benji spun to walk backward along the path. "Miss Levine, can you come with me and Uncle Micah to movie night? It's about a dog and a horse and they're best friends."

That sounded amazing and exactly like how she would enjoy spending her evening. Except it wouldn't be fair to Benji to let him build false expectations about the three of them. "I've got plans, tonight, kiddo. But thank you for asking."

Micah rested a light, restraining hand on her elbow. "Hold on, please. Let's sit over there by the lodge's firepit for a minute before you go."

She frowned. "Because?"

"Because of what you and I were just discussing."

Oh. The book. And he wanted her to be a part

of the discussion? She didn't know how to say no. And she trusted his judgment with Benji. If Micah wanted her to stay for a bit longer, she could manage that. It wasn't like they were alone given all the guests milling about.

Some returning from a hayride in a trailer pulled by a tractor.

Others heading to a wedding reception in one of the barns.

A youth group on a retreat heading to the movie night with corn dogs and popcorn.

"Alright, Benji," she said, gesturing to a bench near the lodge, their cabin and her car in the distance. "Let's sit here, then you can still catch your movie."

She took her place on one end of the wooden seat with paw prints and horseshoes painted along the slats, Benji scrambling up beside her. During the Christmas season, this was the perfect viewing spot, in front of a skating rink and a massive Christmas tree.

And after Christmas Micah and Benji would be gone for good. Would they miss her? She pulled her focus off herself and back to the child.

Micah joined them on the other side of his

nephew. "Hey, Benji, Susanna told me you picked an interesting book at school today."

"Uh-huh." He nodded, his legs swinging. "It was about scaredy-cat dogs. But I'm not a scaredy-cat."

"Well," Micah leaned in conspiratorially, "I am."

"Really?" Benji's feet stopped moving, his blue eyes wide. "Like what? You don't seem afraid of anything."

"When I was a kid, I thought aliens were tapping on my window at night," Micah declared. "But it was just my mother's rosebushes."

Benji giggled.

Susanna couldn't help but be charmed by Micah's effort, so she added, "I was always afraid of getting bad grades in school. And I'm still scared of having all the lights off at night."

Benji laughed, grabbing his sides and rocking on his seat. "You guys are making this up."

Shifting off the bench, Micah knelt, bringing himself to eye level with Benji. "Cross my heart, I'm telling the truth. I wouldn't lie to you."

Benji's smile faded. "But you already did tell a fib."

"I'm not sure what you mean."

The little boy's chest rose and fell faster right before he finally blurted, "You said Grandma and Grandpa couldn't take care of me anymore because they were getting old. But I know they just didn't want me."

Susanna gasped at the pain, the rejection the child had been carrying around. She didn't even know where to begin in saying the right thing. So she simply slid her arm along the back of the bench and gently patted his back.

Micah, on the other hand, did a much better job at hiding his emotions, other than a tiny tic in the corner of one eye. He clasped Benji's hands. "Grandma and Grandpa love you. And they will always want to be your grandparents."

"Then why did they give me away?" The heartbreak in his whisper, the shine of tears in his eyes...

Susanna wanted to gather them both in her arms. But she didn't want to disrupt the moment. She rested her other hand softly on Micah's shoulder as he knelt in front of them.

Micah's throat moved in a long swallow, his Adam's apple bobbing. "They already brought up their children. Now they have a special new job being your grandparents."

Benji's forehead furrowed for a while, then he shook his head. "My mom and dad don't want to bring up me and I'm their kid."

Micah went silent, his pulse throbbing visibly in his temple. He shot a pleading look for help at Susanna.

How could she say no? "Benji, it hurts when people let us down a lot until we can't trust them, and I'm so sorry that has happened to you. And I'm very glad your uncle is here for you. He loves you, and you are never, ever going to have to worry about him letting you down. Okay?"

Benji looked back and forth between them, the tears still clinging. "Uncle Micah? Is what Miss Levine said true?"

"Absolutely. She's a very smart lady." Micah's eyes slid over to her briefly before returning to the boy.

Susanna's heart gave a kick, her tangled emotions for this man growing stronger despite all her best efforts at distance.

Chin quivering, Benji swiped his coat sleeve across his eyes. "You're right about that." He shot to his feet, giving them both a heart-twisting smile. "So can we all go to the movie night now? Together?"

As she looked from Benji to Micah and back again, she realized she couldn't possibly say no—to either of them.

Micah knew Susanna had been guilted into watching the movie with them last week, and that bugged him. Especially in light of his resolve not to take advantage of a woman who seemed to always put others first.

Finally, he'd come up with an idea for a way to thank her, and lucky for him, her friends had been willing to help him on a Saturday while Benji was playing with his friends.

Hands in his jacket pockets, Micah approached the main stable. The musty smell of hay filled his nostrils and horses nickered as they paced in their walkout paddock attached to their stalls. As he approached the heart of the structure, he heard Susanna's soft voice erupt in laughter at something Eliza said.

When he saw them, they were grooming three different horses on the crossties in the center of the stable. "Hey, ladies," he called out to Hollie and Eliza. "Can I steal Susanna away for a while? Once you're done here, of course."

Susanna looked up, startled, fidgeting with the

currycomb in her hand. "Is something wrong with Benji?"

"Not at all," he assured her. "He's hanging out with the O'Brien kids at painting with pets. I would like some time for the two of us to talk— without Benji."

Susanna's gaze locked with his and the air sparked between them in the way that he'd come to accept as inevitable. He waited, giving her time. Hoping he would have this opportunity to thank her. To spend time with her before he moved. He should be done with the project by Thanksgiving— or shortly thereafter—and relocating to the next job site after Christmas.

Grinning, Hollie strolled toward her, hand extended to take Susanna's brush. "We can finish up here."

Susanna handed her currycomb to Hollie, not fully taking her brown eyes off him. She absently stroked the gray mare's neck before turning her attention to Eliza. "If you're sure you don't mind my cutting out early…"

Eliza waggled a horse brush her way. "Have fun."

Susanna bent over to grab her bin of horse cleaning supplies that had been to her left before striding into the tack room. Micah smiled at Hollie and Eliza, who exchanged glances with each other bemusedly.

Emerging from the tack room, Susanna clicked the door shut and followed Micah to the mouth of the stable and then into the yellowed grass outside. "What's going on?"

Micah scrubbed the back of his neck, feeling like a teenager talking to a pretty girl for the first time. "You've done so much for us, I wanted to do something nice for you this afternoon. I asked Hollie and Eliza where I could find you and they made sure you stuck around."

"You could have just asked me."

"I wasn't sure you would say yes. And I really do owe you a thanks for all you've done. So I have a special picnic planned." He held up a hand quickly. "If you would rather not join me, I can absolutely box up the food for you to eat at your leisure."

Her mouth quirked, assessing. She looked past him, indecision forming lines at the corners of her mouth. As she exhaled, she shrugged, golden flecks lighting her deep brown eyes. "You've gone to so much trouble. It would be a shame not to share the meal together. Lead the way."

Relief chugged through him, too much so for such a small thing. Micah opened the passenger door to his truck for her and she climbed in. After closing her inside, he hurried into the driver's seat. With a turn of his key, the truck roared to life. Micah drove toward the main dirt path, dry dust following behind them.

He glanced over at Susanna, who was looking out the window at the falling leaves. "Thanks for sharing your Saturday afternoon with me."

Glancing back at him, she waved dismissively. "I didn't have anything else going on."

He chuckled. "Not exactly a ringing endorsement."

"You know I enjoy our time together," she said softly.

He didn't know that. Not really. But he was glad to hear her say it. He skimmed a silky lock of hair back from her face, tucking it behind her ear. "Me too."

Was it his imagination that she leaned into his hand ever so slightly with a sigh before shifting in her seat?

Susanna toyed with the tail of her braid. "Where are we going?"

"It's a surprise project." He gripped the steering wheel in both hands again, the truck bouncing along the dirt road, trees on either side creating a bower of bare branches. "One I'm really proud of and I thought your students might enjoy as a field trip."

With each passing minute, the forest grew thicker as he navigated the paths toward the feeder pond outside the Sulis Springs cave mouth. Micah stopped the truck fifty feet away from an old red caboose that flanked the pond bank.

The wooden-clad structure had windows running the length of it, a small cupola on top and a roof walk. The rear of the caboose had a small deck with a railing, a ladder nearby leading to the top.

As they both hopped from the truck, he waited for her reaction, feeling like a kid awaiting approval.

Susanna tipped her head to the side inquisitively. "A caboose? I don't recall that being here before."

"It wasn't. I saw it pop up for sale, a real steal. I approached Jacob and Hollie with a plan to convert it into a cabin." He pointed toward the pond near the cave. "I envision a water wheel there to go along with the historic vibe of the train car."

Susanna let out a little squeal of delight, clapping her hands together as her gaze ran over the antique rail car. "What an incredible space this will make. Have you showed it to Benji yet? I bet he'll go crazy over it."

"Not yet. I brought over some sleeping bags, though, to surprise him with a campout." He gestured to the stack of camping gear he'd stashed in the corner. "Since you got him hooked on fairy tales, he's all about the mythical creatures in the woods and the Legend of Sulis Springs."

"I can't wait to hear all about Benji's caboose sleepover adventure." She flipped her braid over her shoulder. "Hollie and Jacob sure chose wisely when they hired you."

"I thought it would make a great feature in the marketing materials, another spot to showcase the unique appeal of this place."

"This will be popular booking. It's so romantic."

The air started crackling again.

He cleared his throat and walked up the steps to the caboose. "Since it's larger than some others I've come across, I drew up a floor plan for making it family friendly."

Micah had already gutted most of the old caboose, although he had left the site spotless—a canvas awaiting its artist's decorative vision. For today, that vision had been his. A table waited by the window, with two chairs and a red checked tablecloth. A picnic basket rested on top.

He'd strung lights throughout, running an industrial electric cord inside for power. He'd installed a small electric fireplace for heat.

Although her approval warmed him more than anything else.

She spun on her heel to stare at him, her fingers gliding along a gilded windowsill.

He gestured, excited to share his vision for this place with her. "The bedroom space will also have room for a crib. And the common space will have a sofa bed as well as kitchenette. But all in deep red velvets and dark panels like the original."

She nodded as he spoke, as if she could see it in her mind's eye too. "It sounds like you really let your imagination run wild."

"You inspired me with how you brought the forest alive with fairy tales."

She'd brought so much warmth and fun back into his life, a feat all the more amazing considering how much stress he'd been under with shoring up his custody of Benji, the financial pressures and, of course, his worries for Benji's transition to a new life while he battled his own struggles. Susanna had been a relief valve for both of them, a bright light in a rough time.

"How are you going to get all of that done before you move? I thought you were already pressed for time since the bear attack."

"The bear attack," he said with a laugh. "I wish the bear attack was all we've had to contend with. After that, a skunk sprayed three of my best workers. A hawk pooped on my blueprints. And a raccoon chewed through the wiring on my favorite circular saw—thank goodness it wasn't plugged in."

It sounded sort of amusing when listed.

"Wow, it seems like the animals are either out to get you," Susanna said, her eyebrow high, "or they're plotting to make you stick around."

His humor faded. "I can't stay much longer. I have to get to work on my next job. But I talked to Jacob and Hollie about coming back here between projects to visit. Benji would have fun seeing everyone. Maybe it wouldn't make goodbye so hard...if we made return trips."

Studying her face, he wondered what she would think, if Susanna would understand she was a large part of him racking his brain for ways to come back here. Would she understand that was part of his surprise too? Not just the caboose or the food, but his need to see her?

He just wasn't ready to say goodbye to Susanna Levine yet.

And before he finished the thought, the caboose door creaked, then slammed shut. What in the world? The wind? He would have to install a hydraulic damper to slow the closing.

"Hold that thought," he said, crossing the caboose. "Let me get my keys out of the lock."

Three strides later, he clasped the doorknob, only to find it was stuck. He rattled the knob and searched through the window. No one was outside. Just a doe sprinting toward the tree line, by the cave.

Coincidence? Or were the animals really conspiring against him again?

Either way, he appreciated the assistance in giving him more time with Susanna.

Frowning, Susanna peered over Micah's shoulder as he jiggled the handle. "What's going on with the door?"

"The knob is stuck." He shook the antique metal hardware gently. "I thought I had the problem fixed, but apparently it needs a bit more of my attention."

Lucky for her he was a master carpenter. A really hunky master carpenter. Currently rocking well-worn denim and a tan suede jacket with a Sherpa collar. "Can you pick the lock?"

"Probably. But it would be easier to take it off the hinges. Thank goodness, I stashed tools in here." He gestured a broad hand toward the table by the window, lights glittering overhead and the small electric fireplace crackling—thanks to the extension cords. "What do you say we eat first?"

Yes. She would say *a big fat yes.* Because time was running out to spend with him and she couldn't find the will to turn down the opportunity for lunch together.

Lunch set up much like a date.

"That would be lovely," she said, peeking into the basket between the two place settings of crockery. "Thank you."

Smoked brisket sandwiches, blue cheese coleslaw, cucumber salad, macaroni and cheese, sweet potato fries and banana pudding. Her mouth was watering.

And then she realized he was holding her seat out for her. "Oh, uh, thanks."

"This is about *me* thanking *you* for the help with Benji and for opening my mind to more creative possibilities at work." He took his seat across from her and lifted out the containers one at a time, filling the table. "Benjamin and I used to play with trains as kids. The little wooden kinds that run on wood tracks. We collected so many, we made villages."

"What a great imagination." He grabbed her plate and carefully doled out each item, before setting it in front of her, perfectly positioned. "That's the teacher in me talking."

"After a while, I realized the ones at the store weren't specific enough for the worlds I wanted to create." Micah dished out his own food, scraping the container with his fork. "So I started carving and whittling. And I was good at it, better than anything I'd done before."

Carving and whittling? She leaned closer, intrigued as she swallowed down a delicious bite of barbecue. "Do you still have some of those trains?"

"I do. They're in a storage unit. I just need to get a break long enough to sort through and find them for Benji. I'd like him to have something positive from his father's childhood." He paused, looking down, moving his coleslaw around on his plate. The lines around his eyes crinkled with worry. "The thing is, Benjamin wasn't always such a screwup."

She reached across the table, resting her hand just shy of him. "Are you okay?"

"Sort of. Not really. Who knows when it comes to my brother." He set his fork down carefully. "I got a call from my folks. They heard from Benjamin."

"How did that go?" Worry scratched around inside her. "Is he causing trouble for Benji? Or for you?"

The thought of him showing up out of the blue again chilled the blood in her veins. How did Micah manage the stress?

"Causing trouble? Always, but nothing I can't handle," he said with a weary sigh. "He told them how upset he is over not getting to see his son and while he was pulling at their heartstrings, he put in a plea to move back in with them."

They couldn't possibly be considering that, especially after refusing to keep Benji. And from what she could see, offering very little support to Micah. Thinking back to Benji's heartbreaking words about being unwanted made her so angry all over again. "What did they say?"

"That he's their son and that he has nowhere to go so he's living in their pool house." With an exasperated wave, he picked up his fork again, skewering some cucumber salad.

So much for being done with parenting as their excuse for not raising their grandson. Thank goodness Micah had legal custody until the adoption could be finalized. "Does Benji know about any of this?"

"No, and the attorney made it clear. If Benjamin's around, my parents can't see Benji either." He plowed a hand through his hair and forced a tight smile. "But enough about that. This lunch is supposed to be about showing my thanks and giving you a fun afternoon out. So, would you like a refill of something? The slaw? The mac and cheese?"

She saw beyond the set of his jaw to the pain in his eyes from his parents' betrayal. She saw to the man grasping at whatever happy memories he could from his childhood and using them to create happiness for others.

Especially for Benji, and for her, too. Looking around at all the effort he'd made today for her sake touched her heart. Propelled her to look beyond the boundaries she'd drawn so rigidly around herself.

Micah wasn't a man like any other. He'd been so respectful of her wishes even though, underneath it all, she saw a man she wanted who desired her too.

And they were running out of time to explore that attraction.

"Well, Micah," she said, clasping his hand and rising from her chair. "What I would really like… is you."

Before he could wipe the stunned look from his face, she slid onto his lap and draped her arms over his shoulders.

Chapter Thirteen

Her scent and softness wrapping around him as tangibly as her arms, Micah stared into Susanna's warm brown eyes fixed right back on him. "I thought we weren't going to do this."

"Me too. I changed my mind. For today, at least. Can we agree that's okay?"

He searched her face and found sincerity...and passion.

Still, he had to be sure she understood. "I didn't bring you here with this in mind. Or rather, let me reword that. Being with you is always on my mind. But it wasn't my intent to take things further than a dinner. I don't want you to feel there was an ulterior motive."

Had he overstepped by prearranging this time with her alone? But the way she leaned into him said she was very much on board with more.

"I know that. I trust you." Her free hand skated across his chest. "You're a man of honor. Otherwise, I wouldn't be sitting here right now, doing my very best to proposition you."

And she was doing an incredible job of it. His heart thudded faster. He'd been ignoring his hunger for her for so long that his brain had a tough time catching up to what his body was already doing. His hand had moved to the small of her back, rubbing circles. Drawing her closer?

He had to take his time and get this right or he would regret it. Susanna was too special. This moment too important. Dragging in a rough breath, he forced himself to slow things down.

"This isn't the sort of place I would have wanted this moment between us to happen," he said, looking around at the makeshift picnic area he'd created inside the caboose. "Let me get the door hinges off and we can go back to my cabin."

"There's no need." She cupped his jaw in her hand, looking into his eyes. "This is the perfect kind of setting with a fairy-tale vibe that stirs my soul. We have history and sleeping bags and curtains over the windows."

He peered at the curtains, seeing her point. But still...

Before he could respond, she tilted her head closer to speak softly in his ear, "And most importantly, I have condoms in my purse."

Her words sent lava through his veins. His fingers flexed against her spine. His mouth went dust dry. "You're sure?"

"Micah?" She teased her fingers along the nape of his neck, just skimming his hairline.

"Yes?" His heart rate double-timed.

"Stop talking," she whispered against his mouth, brushing once, twice, before easing her arms from around his neck. "I'll get the curtains while you spread out the sleeping bags."

She eased from his lap to draw closed the heavy brocade drapes. Moving with speed and purpose, he unrolled the sleeping bags, placing them on top of one another into a fluffy divan with pillows at the head. The electric fireplace blazed nearby. As the drapes slid closed, the space dimmed to just the warm glow of the flames and the tiny lights glinting overhead like stars.

Rising from the bedding, he took in the sight of her as she turned to face him. Slowly, she pulled the fastener from her braid and unplaited the length with a mesmerizing deliberation until her brown locks fell around her shoulders in silky waves.

Leaning against the door, she tugged one ankle boot off and then the other. Every heartbeat knocking against his ribs with the message that this was real. Finally happening.

A low growl of approval rumbled in his chest, echoed by the arousal coursing through his veins. He pulled off his boots, each thudding against the planked flooring. In two long strides, he clasped her hands in his and drew her toward the pillowy softness. She paused only to snag her bag resting by the table on the way past, then dropped it by the makeshift bed.

Urgent need pumped through him, but he wasn't rushing this, not after waiting what felt like an eternity to have her. He drew her into his arms again, sketching his mouth over hers, tasting her. Lingering in the sensation. Sensing that there couldn't be time to get enough.

Kneeling in sync, they sank deeper into the kiss and the puffy sleeping bags. He tucked her closer, her soft breasts pressed to his chest, her foot skimming along his calf. Such a simple gesture and yet so sensuous.

He allowed his hands free rein to roam, to learn the landscape of her hips, her bottom, then up her spine to test the texture of her silken hair. She was everything and more.

And currently unbuttoning his flannel shirt.

He tunneled his hands under her sweater, her satiny skin almost his undoing. Her husky sighs and whispered words of approval flowed against his face. Her fingers encouraged, coaxed, as they drew clothes from each other, taking turns. His shirt, her sweater, his jeans, her leggings.

Her lacy bra.

And so on until they were skin to skin and his brain went on stun. For only an instant.

He hauled her closer. Not nearly close enough. Awash in sensation and a timelessness, melting into the moment, anticipating the moment he could sink into her.

In some dim portion of his mind, he registered her reaching for her bag and coming back with a condom that she passed to him.

"Now? So soon?" he asked, more than ready but not wanting to rush her. He needed this to be incredible for her.

Because he already knew making love to her would be amazing for him.

"Absolutely now. I need you. I need this. Us." She pressed her fingers to his mouth, her beautiful body on full display, pale skin and a freckle on her left breast. "And before you worry, I have more condoms if you would like to take your sweet time next go-round."

Next?

His body shouted a great big yes a second before she tore open the package. He sheathed himself with quick efficiency and tucked her underneath him. He nudged against her, testing, easing inside just as she rolled her hips against him, bringing him deeper. Moving. Each stroke stoking desire higher and hotter.

Her lashes fluttered open and their gazes locked. As her hands played along his back, then gripping lower, he saw himself reflected in her eyes, just as he knew she must be seeing herself in his, a linking that had no end. She met him thrust for thrust, sigh for sigh. She guided him with her hands and breathy gasps. She made no secret of her wants or her pleasure. Which served as an aphrodisiac all its own.

And then his eyes drifted closed and he gritted

his teeth, searching for restraint. Waiting for her, reaching between them to…

Her gasp of completion, her fingernails digging into his shoulders again—and yet again—giving him all the go-ahead he needed to let his own release rock through him. His hoarse shout twining with her sighs.

And even as he rolled to his side and gathered her against his chest, he knew that just having today with her wouldn't be nearly enough.

Susanna didn't regret what she and Micah had done in the train car. Micah had treated her body with passion and tenderness. She'd known the passion was there. Had been prepared for it. Hungry for it.

But the tender care he'd taken with her. That had been her undoing. She wouldn't forget the way he'd checked in with her, making sure he understood what she wanted. Fulfilling every need.

She wouldn't forget that anytime soon. Yet, she wasn't sure how she wanted to handle things between them going forward.

At the touch of a lover, everyone becomes a poet. The Plato quote filtered through her head, reminding her she should probably stop being so poetical about what had happened.

At least as they drove back toward the ranch's main stables to retrieve her car, they both seemed in agreement to keep things light, cracking jokes about prying the hinges off the caboose door.

And only discussing plans for the very near future.

Light danced through the bare branches, dappling their drive back to the main area of Top Dog Dude Ranch. The truck engine rumbled, vibrating her leather passenger side seat as an involuntary smile bloomed across her face. She felt wonderful. Her body well-tended. Her muscles aching pleasantly in ways she hadn't felt in a long time. Even her lips tingled from thorough kissing, a hint of whisker burn at her neck a secret reminder of what they'd shared. Susanna leaned her hand out the window, enjoying the cool air as it fluttered her still-undone braids.

A simple day, the weather having warmed up to the low sixties, temperate enough to enjoy leaving the windows down.

The scent of a bonfire carried along the breeze.

Yet even the most basic conversation was loaded with reminders that their time together was limited. The fast-approaching Wild West themed party would celebrate the completion of the campgrounds. The end of Micah's job here. Although she hadn't missed the implication of his searching for other projects to bring him back, even short term.

What might that mean for them, since Benji wouldn't be a student in her school any longer? Did she dare risk letting the attraction play out?

Questions piled up in her head like library books in a return bin. And searching for answers right now might only steal the afterglow of this day when her body still carried the memory of his touch. Of their chemistry that still had her toes curling.

He draped his wrist over the steering wheel. "What costume have you chosen?"

She trailed her fingers along his jawline, savoring the rasp of his late-day beard. "I'm going as a lady gunslinger, complete with a gun belt slung low on my hips."

She took delight in the surprise on the stark lines of his face. "What were you expecting?"

A safe enough question.

"Maybe a buttoned-up town librarian," he said

with a sheepish shrug. "So are you going as Annie Oakley?"

"Nice guess, but wrong," she said, looking forward to surprising him all over again. "I'll be one of the first female postal carriers in the eighteen hundreds. They made sure the mail was delivered, no matter the conditions. Words matter."

"Now that is a costume your students would love. And a great prompt to go with a book." Micah flipped on his turn signal, guiding the truck toward the wider road leading back. "I can see you riding in a wagon, carrying the mail fearlessly back then."

"Thank you." His words touched her more than they should. "That's an…unexpected compliment."

"You're fierce about helping others—an admirable trait." He looked at her sidelong, those blue eyes threatening to undo her again. Not that there was enough time and space for another encounter as he rounded the next bend, approaching the always impressive main lodge and barns.

A blush heating her face, she shifted the conversation away from herself. "And what about you?"

"My costume is a little simpler. A duster, ten-gallon hat, a leather pouch and a trusty compass. I'm the local cartographer—mapping the terrain, planning towns and making the grids for roads leading in and out."

Micah flashed her a grin that crinkled his eyes as he guided his truck to the stable where he'd picked her up only a few hours ago. Though as she looked at the yellowing grass around her parked car, she felt like their departure had taken place eons ago. So much had shifted in their own geographies.

His answer caught her by surprise—and delighted her too. "Well, that's unexpected too."

"What would you have guessed?"

She let her imagination run as wild as the crisp autumn wind blowing through the cab of the truck. "I could see you as a logger. In fact, that's what I thought of the first time I saw you."

His eyebrows shot up as he slid the truck into an empty parking spot beside her sedan and switched off the engine. "I'm not sure whether to be complimented or insulted."

"In this context," she said, leaning across the truck to kiss him, "it's one hundred percent a compliment."

He cradled the back of her neck, extending the moment to imprint every sensation of their time together, in case there wasn't another chance. She chased even that thought away, reveling in the now.

An unhurried inhale and exhale as his musk and cinnamon scent surrounded her, catapulting her back to the caboose, to the feeling of his arms around her. She pulled away, pressing her lips together in a satisfied smirk.

Micah's throat bobbed, his blue eyes blazing as he leaned forward, mouth parting in a promise.

His phone chimed from the cup holder, bringing a return to reality.

She would have liked to kiss him again, to take her time and even invite him to curl up together in bed. But he needed to pick up his nephew.

And there were people outside the truck.

His cell chimed again.

She unfastened her seat belt. "That's probably Hollie texting about Benji. I should let you go."

"Actually, that's the sound for an incoming email. I've been waiting to hear back about a bid I put in on a big job. Hold on just a second for me to check and then I'll walk you to your car." He tucked a strand of hair behind her ear. "No arguing, please, ma'am."

A bid? On a big job? What a wake-up call that pretending the outside world didn't exist was futile.

As he read, Susanna took in the reality of her hometown. Sometimes it seemed so impossible that she lived here. Children roamed in a small flock, headed for the chicken coop with buckets of feed. Rolling hills tucked this special place in, cloistering the ranch not only from the worst storm systems but also from the rapid pace of overdevelopment happening in so many other mountain regions. She loved this area, the pace, the people.

A low hiss from Micah cut through her thoughts. She turned fast to face him. "Is something wrong?"

"It's an email from the school."

Her stomach knotted. She hadn't expected him to hear anything yet. "What does it say?"

"That they have preliminary findings that do indicate learning disabilities. They want to set up a meeting with his teacher, Mrs. Yoder, the school psychologist and you." He scrubbed a hand along his jaw, his gaze fixed on his cell phone. "They're tossing around words like *dyslexia*, *dysgraphia*. The first, I understand in theory. But the latter? I've never even heard of it."

Oh no. Even though the initial report confirmed what she'd already suspected, it still made her heart hurt for Benji. She knew too well how tough it was for kids to feel different from their peers. But she also knew that early intervention was crucial for academic success. "I promise the school will explain everything and assist you in mapping out the accommodations needed to help Benji succeed."

Exhaling hard, he thumped his cell phone against his knee. "I need that bid to be approved now more than ever."

"Why?" she asked, confused. And more than a little concerned that he wouldn't look at her. "The move will be difficult for him."

"Yeah, but I would have to move regardless." Micah's hand gripped the cell so tightly his knuckles turned white. "The money will be well timed for all the tests and tutors to aid him with the transition."

Concern shifted into something more, like worry with a splash of indignation. Hadn't the man heard anything she'd said these past weeks? "You know there's no substitute for stability and your time. Is it possible to find a work that's closer? We could try a long-distance relationship where I help Benji until you can move back here."

It felt like they were talking at cross-purposes.

Why didn't he understand what she was trying to say? Or at least be willing to discuss compromise?

"Susanna, that's easy enough for you to say, with your parents who were always supportive." Shaking his head, he turned to her, his blue eyes flinty with exasperation. "I'm flying solo here with crummy role models doing the best I can to provide for Benji. Somebody's gotta break the cycle for him, and for better or worse, that somebody is me. He's not living the fairy tales you deal in... this is real life."

His words hurt. Really hurt. She'd swallowed her pride and he'd tossed her offer back in her face.

"Are you breaking the cycle though? Really?" she asked, anger and pain warring inside her as she felt all hope of any future, even short-lived, with this man disappear. As she felt her worries for Benji multiply. "Or are you perpetuating your parents' pattern of paying others to fill in the gaps like your parents did?"

His head snapped back as if she'd slapped him.

And immediately she regretted the accusation. Whether or not there was truth in the words, she wasn't sure. But it had been cruel and impulsive—and she prided herself on being kind and careful.

Not today when her emotions were all exposed.

A shout in the distance made her jolt, her every nerve on edge. Micah frowned just as she realized the loud cry was meant for them.

Hollie was running toward the truck waving. "Wait, wait, please. Benji forgot his backpack."

Susanna blinked, trying to process what her friend had said. "What do you mean? He's with you."

Hollie shook her head. "I just watched him walk to the truck. I saw him come around to Micah's side, just now."

Micah looked out the window, then down at his phone, his eyes going wide.

Horror settled inside Susanna. Benji must have overheard them fighting. He'd possibly even heard them discuss the learning disability. If so, that insecure, fragile boy would be crushed.

What had they done?

Micah threw open the truck door, calling, "Benji? Benji, where are you, buddy?"

But even as she scrambled out onto the dusty earth, she couldn't shake the guilty sense that once again, she'd allowed her feelings to make all the wrong choices. And Benji would be the one to suffer most.

* * *

Micah didn't have time to feel like a failure.

There would be plenty of opportunity for that later.

Right now, he needed to focus on finding his nephew.

They'd only been searching for fifteen minutes, but he was starting to get scared. Starting? Whom was he kidding? He was all-out terrified.

Susanna at his side, he widened his search circle around the barn. Other than calling Benji's name, she hadn't spoken, their disagreement tabled in light of the emergency. Jacob had already made a beeline for the cabin in case Benji had tried to go home.

Home?

His argument with Susanna came crashing down on him again. Her insistence that he was doing the wrong thing by moving again. That Benji wouldn't thrive with more change.

And the weight of that guilt threatened to drive him to his knees at a time he needed to stay focused. Even now as he bounded across the dying grass, his heart raced. In the distance, concerned staff members gathered in small groups. Echoes of his nephew's name clung on the wind.

Familiar faces helped like they were family. The young band singer and the guitarist ran toward the tree line, flashlights in hand in case the search extended past when the sun slunk from view.

He'd never seen anything quite like this. A community pulling together for someone they hadn't known long, and still, they rallied together. The O'Briens had immediately called a halt to all events, launching a full-scale alert.

Even dogs.

Dogs?

Micah tipped his head to the side, tuning into the sound of a puppy barking. And not just any pup.

He stopped abruptly, nearly causing Susanna to trip into him as he tried to orient himself to the bark. Careening his neck to the west, he breathed in a rush of hope and cool air.

Could that be…?

"Jupiter," he shouted, clasping Susanna by the arm, moving toward the yipping. "Jupiter, is that you, pup?"

Another bark cut through the landscape.

Susanna nodded and they both took off running. Lungs burning as he barreled forward, closing in on an old hay wagon. Susanna kept pace, her boots thudding beside him. She pointed at a boot peeking out from underneath the wagon.

Benji.

Micah picked up his pace, running to the back of the wagon, and saw Benji. The boy buried his face in Jupiter's fur, a sob racking the air. Hay mingled in his blond hair, blue eyes red rimmed from the tears streaming down his face. When he spotted Susanna and Micah, he shut his eyes, hugging Jupiter tighter. The pup licked his face.

Relief shot through him so strongly he grabbed the side of the wagon to keep from falling over. He dragged in deep breaths, willing his heart to slow.

"Thank God," Susanna sighed, before pulling out her phone and tapping out texts.

Micah knelt on the ground, peering under the wagon. "Buddy, what's going on? We were worried sick about you."

Another sob caused his body to convulse. He scooted out from the wagon, his lip wobbling as he clung to Jupiter. "I heard what you said. About those tests and how I'm a dummy."

He feared as much. Micah stopped kneeling to sit next to Benji in the dirt. He put an arm around Benji, pulling him close. "That's not true at all."

Benji shook his head. Fresh tears pouring down his face. He blinked, rubbing the tears away with his jean jacket. Benji took a deep breath "But I have a learning disa...diasa..."

Micah swallowed hard and prayed for the right words. "Disability. That doesn't mean you're not smart. In fact, the opposite is true. You are very smart."

"Then what *does* it mean?" Benji scratched Jupiter between the ears, face still twisted in sadness.

Micah looked to Susanna in a plea for help. No matter how angry she might be at him, he trusted she would be there for his nephew.

Susanna lowered herself to take her place on the other side of Benji. "We know that you have trouble reading sometimes. We believe you have something called dyslexia. Now that we understand more about why you've been having difficulty, we can help you figure it out."

"So I'll be able to read better? Will it be hard?" Benji furrowed his brow, his voice losing some of its frantic energy.

"It might be," Susanna conceded. "But there are lots of kids who have a tough time in a subject. It's important to remember that those kids are good at other things. Just like you are good at plenty of things too."

"Like how I know about the planets and the solar system?"

"Exactly." Micah looked at Susanna, her warm eyes working their kind magic once again. He nodded at her and she dipped her chin slightly in encouragement.

Micah cleared his throat. "Benji, where were you going?"

"I was really sad when I heard you guys talk." The boy threaded his fingers through the puppy's fur over and over again. "But then I heard Jupiter barking in the play yard and I thought of the Legend of Sulis Springs." His voice picked up speed. "I thought maybe if I went there I could get healed and you wouldn't give me away."

Just when Micah believed he couldn't feel any lower, the hits kept on coming. He'd failed Benji. In spite of his best efforts. And he had to make that right. "I am never going to leave you. You are my son and I love you. Forever."

Benji shook his head, a strand of hay drifting to the ground. "I love you too, but I'm just your nephew."

He searched for the words to get it right. The

words had to come from him, because if he turned to Susanna now, Benji wouldn't believe him. "You are my son in my heart. And I hope you've seen by now that I keep my promises."

Benji let out a deep breath as Jupiter flipped on her back for a belly rub. He rubbed the white fur of his puppy, his face scrunched in thought. "You know, I think the springs worked even from all this way."

"Why is that?"

"Because Jupiter brought you here." The little boy leaned in to whisper, "I know the Queen of the Forest was supposed to be a deer, but I think maybe this time she was a puppy dog named Jupiter. And she barked so you would know where to find me."

The answer tugged at Micah and he glanced back over his shoulder to share the moment with Susanna. Only to find her gone.

He took another moment to savor the connection with Benji, even as he felt the hurt of Susanna leaving. She'd stayed to help him find Benji because she had a strong sense of duty. Of loyalty. But once Micah had a handle on things, and Benji had stopped being sad, she'd slipped away.

A part of him whispered that he was jumping

to conclusions. But another—far louder—part of him shouted that unless he came up with a miracle, this time she'd given up on him for good.

Chapter Fourteen

The past couple of weeks had been filled with work and heartbreak for Susanna as Micah and his crew completed the campgrounds, while she looked after Benji. And she couldn't ignore the fact they were both staying occupied to keep from acknowledging that their brief opportunity to explore their attraction had passed. They'd barely seen one another, shuttling Benji between them with few words, although they both went out of their way to make polite excuses for the boy's sake.

Now, standing in her Wild West mail carrier garb, she wondered if she was a glutton for punishment, coming to the campground's big-reveal costume party. But pride had propelled her.

Somehow, every event the O'Briens planned always ended up grander than her wildest imaginings. The Wild West party—staged at the completed campground—was lit by torches and campfires. The dense landscape had been preserved, with campsites nestled in tree rings. Even the concrete pads had leaf scrolls imprinted. Half of the sites had been preset with vintage recreational vehicles, open for guests to dine. The other spots sported tents on display, one even with a covered wagon. She kept her eyes off the caboose nestled on the hill in the distance, her heart still too raw from her falling-out with Micah.

Susanna fiddled with the straps holding her faux gun, nerves threatening to get the better of her as she moved toward the grand pine cabin. Warm golden light pooled out of the cabin's large, wide-open double doors, revealing the round tables set for dining and cards, saloon style. The keyboardist from Raise the Woof played tunes on the upright piano.

She scanned the crowd, not even bothering to fool herself that she was looking for anyone other than Micah. A couple dressed as prospectors rushed past her, laughing as they took seats at the saloon table. She strode past the array of decadent food—turkey legs, macaroni and cheese, corn on the cob, fresh-baked corn bread, green beans, mashed potatoes and gravy—the scents making her stomach growl. Nearby, a mother dressed as a sheriff planted a kiss on her toddler's cheek. The red-haired girl laughed, twirling around in her shirt that said "Wanted."

Finally, her gaze landed on Micah, talking with Jacob dressed as a gunslinger standing next to Sheriff Declan Winslow wearing a big tin star. Handsome men, no doubt. But it was Micah who held her captivated, in his black duster and a ten-gallon hat. Sure enough, he had the cartographer's leather pouch and compasses.

Their eyes brushed for a moment, a fraction of a moment, really. She tore her gaze away. Breath caught in her throat as a bit from *Pride and Prejudice* flashed through her mind: "You must allow me to tell you how ardently I admire and love you."

Her cheeks heated at the idea—and the loss.

What she wouldn't give to step into his arms again and dance the night away, lightheartedly enjoying a date night with him. Except nothing between them would ever be simple or lighthearted.

Gripping her coat tighter around her, she backed away from Micah. From temptation. She'd been wrong to come here.

Hollie shouldered her way through the crowd, the maroon skirts of her saloon-girl costume flowing behind her. Her hair was piled in curls on her head, and a thick black shawl draped from her shoulders to her elbows. An elaborate black-and-gold fan dangled from her wrist. "I'm glad you joined us. I feel like we haven't had a free moment to talk since Benji ran off. I still feel so badly he slipped away under my watch."

"No one blames you. It absolutely happens, especially when a kid is determined to sneak off." Although even talking about it made her heart lurch all over again. "And we located him quickly, thanks to a certain pup and the safety protocol you have in place for searches."

At least she and Micah had been able to put aside their differences when it counted. They'd been a good team despite the fear and hurt of that night.

"Thank goodness for Jupiter's bark. It was quite possibly the scariest fifteen minutes of my life."

Hers too.

Benji's words about believing he needed healing had torn right through her. They still did. She'd doubled down to do everything possible to document her notes from tutoring, anything that might help the school psychologist support recommendations for Benji's next school.

Her heart squeezed in her chest again and she searched for something, anything else to take her mind off Micah. "This party is inspired."

Hollie flicked the fan open. The blades extended and she fanned herself, looking like she'd actually stepped out of the 1800s. "I figured you would like the costume angle. We'd considered having this at Halloween, but when we saw the projected completion date, we knew this would be perfect. The caboose is just the icing on the cake."

Susanna almost swallowed her tongue. "Um, right. That was an inspired idea on Micah's part."

Touching Susanna's arm lightly, Hollie steered her to a quiet corner by a watering trough with a horse tied to a post. The light in Hollie's eyes was a little too knowing. "I hope you know I'm a friend and that I care about your happiness. I would love nothing more than for you to live right here in Moonlight Ridge forever, to continue sharing your love of reading with my children…"

"But?" she asked, although not certain she was prepared for the answer.

"The chemistry between you and Micah is apparent to anybody paying even the scantest bit of attention. No one would be surprised if you swapped jobs to be near him."

"I'm not moving," she retorted quickly. "Not again."

And especially not for a man.

She'd already turned her life upside down once. The hurt and betrayal she'd felt had healed, but she wouldn't uproot herself again.

"Do you love him?" Hollie asked too intuitively, then covered her mouth. "Forget I said anything. That's none of my business."

Susanna's breath caught at the question.

"I know you only asked because you care." Yet even as she gave her friend the out, Susanna didn't give her an answer. Not that it stopped realization from rocking through her.

A realization that stole the sparkle from the evening's festivities.

Because she couldn't escape the truth any longer. While yes, she loved little Benji, that wasn't all that tied her heart to their family. She was deeply, fully in love with Micah.

But how could she give her all to a man again who wasn't willing to sacrifice all in return for her?

Micah once hoped that after the campground reveal party was over, he would have the opportunity to spend more time with Benji—and with Susanna before moving on to the next job over in North Carolina.

When Susanna had left the party early, he'd been disappointed, but accepted her texted excuse that she wasn't feeling well. Yet even after that, it felt like she was avoiding him, day after day, just counting down the hours until he moved. When he came to the school, she was all business, which was understandable. However, he couldn't miss how after tutoring Benji, she made a point of clearing out the instant Micah crossed the cabin doorstep.

But at least he could finally hang out with his nephew more often.

Parked in the ranch's workshop with Benji, Micah put the finishing touches on his farewell gift for Susanna. She'd left such an imprint on their lives, he'd searched for at least some small way to leave her a reminder of their time together as well.

Micah rearranged the scattered tools that had piled on the workbench. He hung the hammer from a pegboard in the rustic shop, inhaling deeply. Fresh-cut wood scented the air. He plucked up screws, placing them in the appropriate bins while the overhead light hummed.

At the edge of the bench, he found where he'd set his paintbrush. He picked it up, spinning the wood handle in his fingers. The space was blessedly deserted today, other than him and Benji, and the low hum of Christmas music. Jupiter snoozed on his dog bed, leash secured.

Benji sat on a bar stool, feet swinging as he ran a piece of sandpaper back and forth over a block of wood that would offer the finishing touch to their project.

Micah had built a large doghouse designed to be a reading station for children. He dipped his brush into the lime green, the color he'd used to trim the doghouse windows. Robin egg blue warmed the inside of the doghouse reading room. He'd ensured that there'd be room for a couple of beanbag chairs inside. A perfect reading nook. One Benji had enjoyed while Micah had worked on this project the past few days.

Benji placed the sandpaper on the table. "Why don't you and Miss Levine talk anymore?"

"I saw her when she and I met with the school about the plan for helping you with reading." A meeting that confirmed Benji's diagnosis and spelled out a plan for his new school when they relocated. "And I see her every day since she tutors you," Micah said evasively, the question sending a pang through him.

He couldn't stop thinking about her. Wondering what he should have done differently that night they'd argued. He'd done his best to put on a good front for Benji over Thanksgiving, even though he felt hollow inside.

"But you don't talk to each other." Benji held his block up to the light, admiring it for a second before shaking his head. "Not like you used to."

The kid was too insightful. But Micah had learned that hiding concerns and problems hadn't kept the boy from worrying. Better to share as much as was appropriate for a child his age. And the truth of the matter? Micah was miserable. He missed Susanna more than he could have expected and he hadn't even moved yet.

Pausing to pin his entire focus on Benji, Micah leaned against the workbench. "You know it's time for us to leave for North Carolina after Christmas. We'll be saying goodbye to everyone here."

He'd already stayed at the ranch longer than he'd originally planned.

Benji set aside his sandpaper and wooden block, his jaw trembling. He reached into his pocket and pulled out a folded piece of paper. "I wrote Miss Levine a poem. Well, I mean, I wrote it with Ivy's help. We talked about it and she spelled everything." He opened the page, clutching it in his hands to read,

"Ms. Levine is a queen.

She knows fairies in the evergreen.

And she is magic.

and she taught me to dream.

Thank you. Love, Benji."

Micah pulled over a bar stool for himself, surprised and more than a little choked up. "Benji, that's really great. I'm sure she'll love it."

"She really likes poems." Blushing, Benji folded up the paper again and slid it back into his jeans. "She read me a poetry book this one time, and it was all about words that sound the same. I can hear the sounds, even if I can't read them. That's why I needed Ivy's help."

"I'm impressed." And he truly was. Thinking of

how far the boy had come already, after so much adversity? Even more impressive, Benji still had such a boundless capacity for love. Micah was humbled.

Grabbing the block of wood again, Benji ran his fingers over his work, testing the smoothness. "I did it because of Miss Levine." He traced over the letters that Micah had whittled out to spell A-T-L-A-S. "Except she said I can call her Susanna now that I'm not going to be her student anymore."

"How do you feel about that? About her no longer being your nanny?" Even as he said the words, he knew the answer and that it wouldn't make him happy.

"Really rotten." He kept tracing the letters dejectedly.

"Me too," Micah admitted.

"So how come she can't stay with us?"

The last thing he wanted was to betray Susanna by telling Benji she wouldn't leave. Not that he'd even asked her. "Because we are moving. And she lives in Moonlight Ridge."

"We could stay here, because we love her and that's what we need to do to be with her," he said with the unerring simplicity of a child.

Yes, definitely too insightful. The realization

that Benji saw right through him to his true feelings for Susanna made him wonder all over again how he'd get through this move.

"I wish we could, buddy." And he found that to be true. This was a magical place, not just because of Moonlight Ridge or the Top Dog Dude Ranch. But because Susanna was here, and yes, he loved her. However, it would be a long while before he could build his business to a level that allowed him to put down roots while sending crews out. "But it's not that simple. My job means I have to travel. And you and I are a team. We stick together, always."

"Sure." He nodded somberly. "But do you think if you tried really, really hard, you could learn how we wouldn't have to say goodbye to her? I worked really, really hard and I wrote a poem. That's something nobody thought I could ever do."

The kid was killing him. And he had a point.

"Sometimes in life, trying hard just isn't enough."

Like with Benjamin overcoming addiction. Or their parents' inability to step up to help with Benji, yet enabling their son's drug habit.

Benji tugged his arms into his sweatshirt, a mischievous smile spreading across his face. "Sounds to me like you're not using your imagination."

Such a simple statement.

Yet, as the words rolled over him again in his mind, so utterly brilliant.

Could it really be that he'd been so locked in on an absolute fix, like a blueprint, that he'd lost all sight of the creativity required for compromise that Susanna had asked him to look for? Had he been like Benji, afraid of being let down because of his parents and Benjamin? So much so that he hunkered down as an island, shutting out input from others?

Even entertaining the notion felt like someone had opened doors in his mind, letting in sunlight and possibility. Bits of ideas sparkled. Would all those glimmers of inspiration work out? Probably not. But he only needed one. And he was determined to find that gem. Because he loved Susanna and he didn't want to lose her.

And thanks to Benji, he thought he might finally have found a path through to winning her back.

For good.

"Benji, what do you say we put our heads together on a little project for Susanna?"

* * *

Inside Micah's cabin, Susanna gathered her bag and Atlas's toys, trying not to dwell on the fact this had been her last day tutoring Benji. Even though they hadn't moved yet, her contract as his after-school nanny was officially complete and it felt wrong to let Benji grow any more attached to her.

She tossed a dog bone in the sack. Cleaning anchored her. Well, at least it gave her somewhere to put the nervous energy dancing in her chest. Susanna grabbed the snack plates and snack wrappers on the cabin's kitchen countertop. She'd been struggling with tears since she woke up, feeling hopeless, but trying to stay upbeat for Benji. Clearly, he was excited about something. Thankfully, Benji hadn't picked up on her mood, already brimming with holiday spirit a bit early. He spun and spun and spun in the living room. His reindeer and dog Christmas sweatshirt a green blur and Jupiter trailed around. Three burlap stockings were hung from the fireplace, labeled Micah, Benji and Jupiter. A small tree with lights rested on the table, with four presents already wrapped and waiting.

Benji stopped spinning, stumbling her way. "That gift right there is from me to you." He leaned in to whisper, "And the card on top of it has a poem I wrote for you. For real."

A poem? A fresh batch of tears burned her eyes. "Thank you so much. Should I open it now? Or do you want me to take it home?"

Benji grinned, his energy irrepressible. "How about leave it right there for now. There's more to your surprise. We are supposed to meet Uncle Micah at the workshop. Come on. I'll lead the way."

He tugged on his coat, then tucked his sticky little hand into hers, much the way he'd nestled into her heart. With her spare hand, Susanna swiped the two dog leashes that hung to the right of the door. She knelt, clipping Atlas and Jupiter. Benji helped push open the cabin door and they stepped out into the dwindling daylight, cool air flooding her senses.

A final walk to the woodshop Micah had been using. Suddenly, her limbs felt a bit numb, regret over how things had been left between them consuming her thoughts as she crossed the length of two yards.

"Uncle Micah, we're here," Benji shouted with all the volume and force of a six-year-old with a secret.

Susanna stopped in the doorway, letting the dogs run ahead inside with Benji. Adjusting to the warm, steady light of the workshop, she looked around at the carefully stowed tools. Her eyes falling on a big doghouse at the room's center. "Atlas" was hand painted in a stunning script font on the one of the boards. Bright colors and the fanciful design told her this was not just for her but for her students too. A fun haven for children.

Susanna's mouth went dry, stunned. "The doghouse is beautiful. Thank you."

Did these two males have to keep putting her emotions through the wringer? It would already be tough enough to say goodbye.

Micah stepped out of the shadows, all broad shoulders and big heart. "For your library. I thought it would work when you have story time with Atlas at school."

She couldn't take her eyes off him, remembering all they'd shared. How much she'd come to look forward to seeing him every single day.

And now this.

A big, beautiful gesture. One that ensured she thought of him every day.

Benji dropped her hand, bolting inside. "See? It's great for reading." He grinned. "Or for watching my tablet. Uncle Micah said I could have extra screen time if I let you guys talk."

And apparently, he'd planned for this since the device was already stashed in the doghouse. Benji put on his headphones and settled into a movie with the dogs.

Susanna turned to face Micah again. "I can't believe this wonderful gift. Thank you so much."

"Benji was as excited to share it with you as I've been. It's been a good project for us." He moved closer to her.

Her mouth went dry. "You wanted to talk to me?"

"I wanted to show my appreciation for all you've done for Benji."

"I'm only doing my job," she said, seeing in his deep blue eyes she wasn't fooling him any more than herself.

"I also wanted you to see where I work. Who I am. Because, I think I'd lost sight of it. I like to work with my hands. My world is so very different from yours."

"But your creativity—"

"Yes, I'm getting to that. Since you like the creative angle of the doghouse for your library, what do you think of a reading loft in your library—all built to code, of course." He led her to a bench, the ends shaped like the silhouette of a dog. A wooden tree was in the works off to one side, carved little animals lined up underneath.

Carving?

He'd begun carving again.

Her legs folding, she sat on the doggy bench. "I think that sounds magical." Perfect actually. But she didn't understand why he was doing all of this. Out of guilt because he was moving? "You don't have to do all of that for me."

"I know I don't have to. I want to show you I've learned how to blend our worlds, thanks to you. Your library and my workshop. And I think our worlds—we—look good together."

And as his words sunk in, a trickle of hope flowed through her, the possibility that he hadn't brought her out here just to give her a farewell Christmas present.

She'd missed him so. But she needed to know how they would make this work, because she wanted it to, more than she could have imagined. "So you're proposing that we give a long-distance relationship a try like I suggested?"

She'd been so miserable without him, she ached

to find a solution that honored who they each were. Was that what he was trying to tell her?

"Long distance? I don't know about you, but these past weeks without you have been some of the worst of my life. I don't want to spend any more time apart." He took his place beside her, clasping her hands in his. "I've reached out to some subcontractor buddies of mine to see if they can take on the North Carolina project. I'll work some smaller gigs here while I hammer out long term business plans."

"That simple?" she asked breathlessly.

"Not quite simple," he answered with a wry chuckle. "But doable as long as I consult on the side."

She could hardly believe her ears or the offer he'd made. "Micah—"

"Hold that thought." He traced her lips quiet. "I know this may seem crazy soon, but I want to build more than a reading loft for you. I want to build a life with you. And whatever compromises I have to make for that to happen, including putting down roots here in Moonlight Ridge, I'm all in."

Move here? For her? Her heart fluttered. "But you need to move to grow your construction company. That's your dream."

"Susanna, you are my dream." He skimmed a hand over her hair to cradle her face. "I've fallen in love with you, and I hope you'll give me the chance to show you just how much. Will you give me that chance?"

She clasped his declaration close to her heart. How had she not seen the possibilities before now? Somehow, she'd let her past relationship cloud her judgment. She'd told others to let their imaginations run wild and envision the impossible.

But all this time she'd had tunnel vision when it came to this incredible man.

Now, it was time to start following her own advice. Excitement blossomed inside her. "Under one condition."

"What would that be?"

"That we plan how that relationship looks together. Creatively."

He grinned, teasing a lock of hair between his fingers. "Deal."

A full smile pulled at her mouth and heart in response. He was offering so much more than she'd expected, relocating for her, while including opportunities for adventures. Together. She promised herself she would find ways to compromise too. To make his life easier.

Touched, she tipped her forehead to his. "I like the way you think. And even more than that, I like you. In fact, I have fallen in love with you too."

"I'm so very glad," Micah said as a sigh of relief shuddered through him, speaking to her far more than any words about how much this meant him—how much she meant to him.

She skimmed her fingers up his chest, twisting in his padded flannel shirt and tugging him closer. "How long do you think our three little matchmakers over there will keep watching the movie?"

His mouth a breath from her, mischief in his eyes. "Let's find out."

Epilogue

Six months later

Though she be but little, she is fierce.

The Shakespearean line had officially become Micah's favorite quote. And it was easy enough to remember too since it reminded him of the love of his life.

He never tired of seeing Susanna, hearing her. Late-spring sun shone through the trees, glistening off her braid as she sat on a quilt reading to a group of children from the Top Dog Dude Ranch.

Today marked the celebration of the grand

opening of the water wheel he'd constructed in the moving water outside Sulis Springs cave. The caboose gleamed with a fresh coat of paint at the tree line, sparking memories of his first time making love to Susanna. A pleasure he'd had the opportunity to repeat often over the past six months. He suspected sixty years wouldn't be enough.

He'd already arranged for a supper to be waiting inside the finished rail car today. The perfect place to propose. An engagement ring box was currently burning a hole in his pocket even now. Hollie had helped him pick out the princess-cut diamond and made sure he had the right size.

But he savored this quiet moment of anticipation, observing the woman he loved with her little charges. Atlas was curled up on her lap. She had read a storybook to the kids about water wheels and now took their questions. Benji sat on the back row hugging his knees alongside Ivy and the O'Brien boys.

Susanna sat cross-legged, the children's book propped in front of her. "The force of the moving water pushes against the paddles, which is then used to set the machinery into motion."

"Why not just plug in the cord?"

"Maybe they aren't supposed to play with electricity, dummy," a child called from the front row.

Benji stood up, hands on his hips. "We don't call people *dummy*. That's a bad word."

Susanna smiled at Benji. "You're right. *Dummy* is not a word we should ever call another person"

Ivy chimed in, "They used their imaginations and figured out about the water and its power."

The distinctive sound of a camera shutter clicked softly, the lens from a photographer trained on Susanna as she led the group. A TV news crew filmed as well. He'd expected his plan to anchor his business in Moonlight Ridge to necessitate a pay cut. Instead, his work at the ranch had generated such a buzz in other regions, he now ran subcontracted crews around the country.

And it was all thanks to Susanna.

She continued to tutor Benji, but she'd also started her master's degree. She was a firecracker, ready to set the world on fire. Her students were lucky to have her.

He was lucky to have her.

In her typical way of sharing the limelight with others, she turned over the presentation to Jacob and Hollie, who would be leading the kids in a close-up tour of the wheel and springs inside the cave.

And Susanna had written the educational story she'd shared with the children. The project had started when she compiled the tale using words Benji needed. Now, copies of her books were sold in the Top Dog gift shop.

Susanna stood. "As you make a line to follow Mr. and Mrs. O'Brien, be sure to tell them some other things we read about that were helped by building a wheel."

Answers piled one on top of the other.

"A paddleboat and you use your feet?"

"Wooden wagon wheels?"

"A chariot pulled by a horse?"

"Gears in a clock are wheels that hook together."

Micah held out his arms for Susanna as she darted around the quilt and into his embrace. He spun her around. "You were incredible."

"I had good material to work with," she said, pointing toward the wheel. "I love how the final product turned out."

The wooden wheel churned water outside the cave opening as the small TV crew followed eagerly behind the O'Briens who were dressed in matching plaid shirts. Children trailed behind them, whooping with wonderment as the wheel funneled more water into the cave opening.

"We make a pretty good team." He skimmed a kiss over her mouth, passion stirring. "If you're free, I have dinner waiting for us in the caboose."

She looked longingly at the painted red rail car, then back at him. "What about Benji?"

Linking his hand with hers, he squeezed. "I appreciate how much you love that kid. Really, I do. But he's been begging to go camping with the O'Briens in one of the vintage campers."

The kids had been asking to use the latest gnomes, fairies and creatures that he'd whittled. The gift shop was carrying some of those figurines now too. Their world truly was full of creativity... and love.

Susanna's eyes glistened with delight. "So we have all night to ourselves?"

"Yes, ma'am, we do."

"Well, that's a lucky turn." She led him up the caboose steps, promise in her eyes. "Because I've been thinking tonight might be the night I propose and make an honest man out of you."

Throwing his head back, laughter rolling free, he scooped her up and carried her over the threshold for the start of their very own forever fairy tale.

* * * * *

Be on the look out for the next
Top Dog Dude Ranch book,
coming October 2022,
from Harlequin Special Edition!

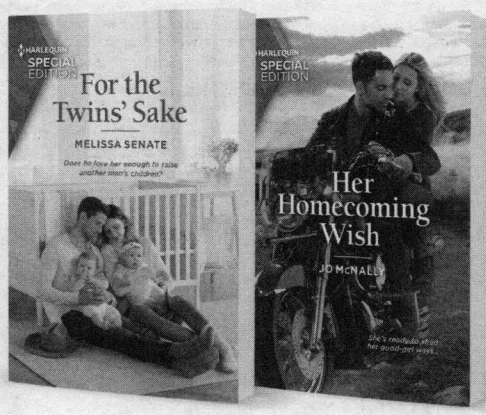

COMING NEXT MONTH FROM

HARLEQUIN
SPECIAL EDITION

Stationed in her hometown of Port Serenity, coast guard captain Skylar Beaumont is determined to tough out this less-than-ideal assignment until her transfer goes through. Then she crashes into Dex Wakefield. She hasn't spoken to her secret high school boyfriend in six years—not since he broke her heart before graduation. But when old feelings resurface, will the truth bring them back together?

Read on for a sneak peek at
Sweet Home Alaska,
the first book in USA TODAY *bestselling author Jennifer Snow's Wild Coast series.*

Everything looked exactly the same as the day she'd left.

Though her pulse raced as she approached the marina and the nondescript coast guard station, her heart swelled with pride at the sight of the *Starlight* docked there. With its deep V, double chine hull and all-aluminum construction, the forty-five-foot response boat was designed for speed and stability in various weather conditions. Twin diesel engines with waterjet propulsion eliminated the need for propellers under the boat, making it safer in missions where they needed to rescue a person overboard. Combined with its self-righting capability to help with capsizing in rough seas, it had greater speed and maneuverability than the older vessels. The boat was the one thing she had total confidence in. And she would be in charge of it and a crew of five.

The crew was the tougher part. She was determined to gain their trust and respect. She was eager to show that she was one of them but also maintain a professional distance. Her father and grandfather made it look so easy, but she knew this would be her hardest challenge, to command a crew of familiar faces. People she'd grown up with, people who remembered her as the little girl who'd wear her father's too-big captain hat as she sat in the captain's chair in the pilothouse.

Did that hat finally fit now?

Weaving the rental car along the winding road, and seeing the familiar Wakefield family yacht docked in the marina, her heart pounded. The fifty-footer had always been the most impressive boat in the marina, even now that it was over thirty years old. Its owner, Kurt Wakefield, had lived on the yacht for twenty-five years.

Kurt had died the year before. Skylar peered through the windshield to look at it. Had someone else bought the boat? Large bumpers had been added to the exterior, and pull lines could be seen on deck. She frowned. Had it been turned into some sort of rescue boat?

It wasn't unusual for civilians to aid in searches along the coast when requested, but the yacht was definitely an odd addition. There had never been a Wakefield who had shown interest in civil service to the community…except one.

The man standing on the upper deck now, pulling the lines. Wearing a pair of faded jeans and just a T-shirt, the muscles in his shoulders and back strained as he worked and Skylar's mouth were dry. She slowed the vehicle, unable to look away. Almost as if in slow motion, the man turned and their eyes met. Her breath caught as familiarity registered in his expression.

And unfortunately, the untimely unexpected sight of her ex-boyfriend—Dex Wakefield—had Skylar forgetting to hit the brakes as she reached the edge of the gravel lot next to the dock. Too late, her rental car drove straight off the edge and into the frigid North Pacific Ocean.

Don't miss
Sweet Home Alaska,
available May 2022 wherever
HQN books and ebooks are sold.

HQNBooks.com

"Now, I know the circumstances aren't ideal, but I'ı
looking forward to working with you."

She appeared to struggle, like she was thinking hov
to formulate her words. "I wish I was working with yo
by choice and not circumstance. Not that I would choos
to," she said with a chuckle.

"I hear you. If it weren't for this situation, we woul
still be throwing daggers at each other during leadersh
meetings."

"Put yourself in my shoes. If you were going throug
this, how would you feel?" she asked, rubbing her t
into the carpet. "Honest answer."

"I'm not as brave as you are, and I have more pri
than common sense."

She blushed and averted her eyes. "I would have resigned if I didn't have a mother and sister to consider. Pride is secondary to priority."

He felt ashamed and got to his feet. He went over to her. "You're right. I'm thinking like a single man. If I were married or had other responsibilities, I'd do what I'd have to and keep my job. I was hoping that Irene—" He stopped, unsure of the etiquette of bringing another woman into the conversation.

"No need to stop on my account. I know you had—have—a life."

Lynx wasn't about to talk about Irene, no matter how cool Shanna claimed she was with it. "I'm ready to fall in love, get married and install the white picket fence."

"How do you know you're ready?" she asked.

He rubbed his chin. "I'm at the brink of where I want to be professionally. I want someone to share my success with me."

"I get it," she said, doing that half-bite thing with her lip again.

Don't miss
Rivals at Love Creek
by Michelle Lindo-Rice,
available July 2022 wherever
Harlequin Special Edition books and ebooks are sold.

Harlequin.com

HARLEQUIN

Heartfelt or thrilling, passionate or uplifting—Harlequin is more than just happily-ever-after.

With twelve different series to choose from and new books available every month, you are sure to find stories that will move you, uplift you, inspire and delight you.

SIGN UP FOR THE HARLEQUIN NEWSLETTER

Be the first to hear about great new reads and exciting offers!

Harlequin.com/newsletters